Love's Tender Portrait

Love's Tender Portrait

ALICE SHARPE

AVALON BOOKS
THOMAS BOUREGY AND COMPANY, INC.
401 LAFAYETTE STREET
NEW YORK, NEW YORK 10003

AAQ4421

PRINTED IN THE UNITED STATES OF AMERICA
ON ACID-FREE PAPER
BY HADDON CRAFTSMEN, SCRANTON, PENNSYLVANIA

AUG 27 1991

For my brother, Phillip LeVelle

Chapter One

LILA tenderly wrapped the last piece of Limoges china in tissue paper and stacked it in the big cardboard box with the other one hundred and four pieces. She'd always thought that someday she would serve special dinners to her husband on these plates, or mash a Christmas banana for her first child in one of the gold-rimmed bowls. But they weren't to be hers, after all, and as she turned away from the box and looked at the newly gutted room, she felt a fresh dose of sadness swell in her throat.

The sound of the doorbell cut it short. She swallowed and crossed the room with determined strides, and by the time she opened the front door, she had managed to dredge up a smile and plant it firmly on her face.

"Miss Greene," the real estate agent said. "I know we're a little early, but—"

"It's okay," Lila said. "Come in."

Ray Bauer was on the far side of fifty, a good-looking man with a smooth smile and ruffled hair. He nodded at Lila as he ushered in a new set of potential buyers, this time a middle-aged couple. Lila was momentarily diverted by the fact that these two people looked almost exactly alike, so she didn't hear the first part of the sentence Ray directed her way.

"—so we won't be a moment," he finished.

"What? Oh, I see. That's okay."

"Lovely house," the woman said, her words uttered through plump lips painted cadmium red. "Don't you think so, Father?"

"Did this house belong to *the* Constance Greene?" the man asked.

"Yes, it . . . it did," Lila said.

"Tragic thing, her dying of cancer like that," the man said. "So young, really. Maybe not to you, young lady, but to folks like us—"

"And right in the middle of her career," the woman added. "Think what she might have done if she'd lived longer!"

The real estate agent must have noticed how the couple's words were about to plunge Lila into a sea of despair, for he moved quickly through the end door and said, "Right this way, Mr. and Mrs. Row. The kitchen is through here. You're going to love the delightful little sketches Constance Greene made on the walls and the. . . ."

His voice trailed away. Lila headed in the opposite direction, ending up in her aunt's studio. She closed the door behind her and leaned back against it. After a moment or two she wiped her face dry on the tail of her flannel shirt and took a deep, steadying breath.

Lila thought the studio was the best room in a fascinating house. The windows were floor-to-ceiling on the north side, café-curtained and shuttered to control the light. Along the south wall was the model's stand, in reality no more than an eighteen-inch-high plywood box measuring forty-eight by forty inches. A short flight of stairs led up to the platform, and for an instant Lila was transported back twenty years when, as an excited four-year-old, she climbed those steps to pose for Aunt Connie.

Even then, Lila thought now, she'd realized two things. One was that Aunt Connie at the ripe old age of twenty-five, was special, a talent in the making, an erupting force in the art world that people were beginning to respect. The second thing Lila knew, even when she was four, was that she was more like her aunt than like her own mother.

She looked away from the stand, her gaze automatically drifting to the west wall, where faded rectangles marked the places Constance's favorite paintings had once hung. Like the dishes, the few good pieces of furniture, the car, and the house itself, the paintings had been given in a living will to Lila before Constance died so that Lila wouldn't be tied up with probate after the event.

The paintings had already been sold; the furniture was at the auctioneers', where the dishes were soon to be sent; the car was gone, picked up by a man for his seventeen-year-old son. And the house wouldn't last long. If the Rows didn't realize what a buy it was, the next couple would. All the proceeds would go to whittle away the astronomical debts Constance had accumulated over the last two years of her life, debts that now belonged to Lila. Toward this goal, Lila had even been forced to sell a few of her own paintings, and though they didn't fetch near the price her aunt's had, every penny, as the lawyer was fond of pointing out, helped.

Now, against that once-treasured wall were piled the odds and ends of the studio—three chairs, a small love seat, a wicker bench, a background screen, two old easels, and half a dozen discarded paint boxes. Some of this would find its way into the trunk of Lila's car; some would go to the Salvation Army with the rest of the household furniture that was too bulky to keep and too nondescript to sell.

In the middle of the room stood a huge paint stand that supported a thick glass palette. Lila crossed to the stand. An easel sat beside it, and for an instant she saw her aunt at work, the brush dabbing into the paint, then making quick trips to the canvas, where sure strokes created such magic.

The painting presently occupying the easel helped with this impression, as it was of Constance Greene herself, a half-finished portrait of a beautiful woman ravaged by disease until the only thing left to blaze were her black eyes. Lila had tried to catch the mixture of hope, anger, resignation, and love that permeated the eyes, burning through the fatigue, leaping now off the canvas as a firm challenge to Lila not to dwell in self-pity. The unfinished work was signed because her aunt had demanded that Lila do so. ''I want to see you sign it, darling,'' she'd said at the end of what was to be her last lucid day. ''Humor me—sign it now.''

Had Constance somehow known that she would deteriorate during the night, that for all intents and purposes, unless Lila wanted to work from memory, the painting was complete?

Why did I escape into this room of all rooms? Lila thought. She yanked open the studio door and came face-to-face with Ray.

''Just going to show Mr. and Mrs. Row the studio,'' he said.

Lila stood aside. ''Of course.''

The Rows moved into the room as though it were a sanctuary, and Lila thought, *Good. At least they'll respect it.*

''By golly, Mother, but wouldn't this make a dandy playroom?''

''You mean with a pool table and a wet bar?'' Mrs. Row said.

Lila and Ray exchanged startled looks; then Lila turned on her heels and left. The last thing she heard Mrs. Row say was, ''Look at this painting. Who'd want to paint someone who looked like that?''

The last of the packing was done. For the first time in two years Lila was emotionally free to leave, to choose what to do next, and she hoped, she fervently hoped, that the prospect would appeal to her more as time went by. Two years before, upon graduation from art school, she'd had three job offers, all of which she'd turned down. She could still recall the moment—under maple trees, diploma in hand—when Aunt Connie had come clean with her health problems.

It had marked the transition from childhood to womanhood for Lila, the moment when she went from taker to giver. The jobs were long filled, and Lila had no idea if there would be others waiting, but of one thing she was certain—she didn't regret for one moment her decision to put her own life on hold so that Aunt Connie could end hers in her own home, working as long as possible, creating and challenging herself until she was too weak to hold a paintbrush.

Then Lila had taken over for her, finishing the last of a series of paintings commissioned by a bank, assuring the two members of the board of directors that their portraits would fit in with the ones her aunt had already completed. And they had too. In many ways Lila felt as though she'd learned more about portrait painting in the last two years than she had during college.

She was sitting on the hearth, looking at another portrait she'd painted of her aunt, this one done the previous spring before things had gotten so bad, when she heard the bell ring. She opened the door quickly and found Ray Bauer. She looked behind him, but he seemed to be alone.

"May I come in?" he asked.

"Of course."

They stood in the living room for a few moments, Lila unsure what to say.

"I know this is hard for you," Ray said, scratching the top of his head.

She nodded, his hesitation making her uneasy.

"I wanted to tell you myself because over the last few weeks I've grown to . . . well, to admire you." Lila looked up quickly and he added, "I mean, I think you're handling things so well. . . . This isn't coming out right."

"What did you want to tell me yourself?" she asked.

He sighed deeply. "The Rows will pay you exactly what you asked. Cash. They wanted to make a smaller offer, but I told them you wouldn't even consider it, that the housing market might be a little sluggish in San Francisco but this house is special. I guess I was being rather unprofessional, kind of hoping they'd get discouraged and give up on it so you'd have a little longer to live here, but there you are."

"The whole asking price?" Lila repeated.

"Every dime."

She nodded, knowing she should breathe a deep sigh of relief. The money from the house would pay off most of the bills. If the dishes and the other things at the auctioneers' fetched what they were worth, she'd soon be free and clear. So why did she feel like sitting on the floor and crying?

"Thank you," she said woodenly.

"Lila—"

"I really appreciate it," she added.

"Do you have somewhere to go?" he asked.

"Oh, sure," she lied, not about to confide that she was darn near penniless and now homeless.

His eyes strayed to the portrait on the wall behind Lila's head. "She was some woman," he said. "You must miss her terribly. I know it's been a couple of months now, but I hear you were very close, that you were like her in many ways—"

"Yes," Lila interrupted, his compassion making things harder. "But I had more of her than anyone else in the world," she added. "I should be grateful for that too."

He nodded. "And you have this portrait of her. I see the name Greene on the bottom. Was it a self-portrait?"

Lila turned around, the familiar face on the canvas reassuring her. "No, I did it," she said.

"You did? Well, well."

"It's to go to the City by the Sea Museum," she added. "They're mounting a show of her early work. I should have sent it over long before, but. . . ."

"Yes, I think I see."

"Thanks. Tell the Rows they've got themselves a house. I'll be out in two weeks."

"There's no need to rush. Even with cash, escrow will take a month—"

"I want to get going," she said. Truth of the matter was, she couldn't afford staying in the house another month.

He shook her hand and was gone. Lila went back to the studio, imagined it as the Rows' playroom, and said a silent apology to her aunt.

* * *

The Salvation Army truck pulled away from the curb two weeks later. Lila locked the doors and put the key in the mail slot as she'd told Ray she would. She turned around just as the mail truck pulled up at the end of the walk.

"So you're moving," the mailman said as he spied her two suitcases and the paint box with the folding easel strapped to the outside.

"The house sold," she told him.

"It's not going to be the same," he said as he handed her two letters. "Your aunt was a fine woman."

Lila smiled. "Yes," she agreed.

"You take care of yourself, young lady. I've seen some of your paintings—Constance showed them to me. You're good. Shame you couldn't have stayed right here in this house and used her studio—"

"Things just didn't work out," Lila interrupted softly.

He nodded. "Sometimes they don't, that's right. Well, be sure to send your change of address to the post office. Good luck to you."

Lila waved good-bye as the mailman drove down the tree-lined street. She looked at the top envelope and saw that along with half the adult population of the United States, she might be the lucky winner of ten million dollars. She looked at the second envelope and saw "Miss Greene" written in flourishing script.

Lila opened the second envelope and withdrew a folded piece of expensive lilac-colored and scented stationery. She read:

My dear Miss Greene,

I am hereby commissioning you to paint my portrait, even though Steven assures me this is not the way it's done. I don't know what you charge for this honor, but since I hear you're the best, I'm prepared to pay it. As I no longer travel, I trust you will come to me. Enclosed is my address near San Diego, where I have a little cottage by the sea. Also enclosed is a check to be used as a deposit. If for some reason you cannot paint my portrait, I expect you'll return the check, because if you don't, it will mess up my accounts and Steven will have a fit. Come at once as my birthday is on the eighth, and wouldn't it be nice if you were finished by then?

Yours sincerely,
Endora Yolette

For one awful minute Lila felt a stab of loss as acute as a knife twisting in her heart. How she and Aunt Connie would have chuckled over this letter! She shook away the pain and laughed out loud, the first laugh she'd tried in months. It sounded a little shaky, but kind of nice too, and she could almost see Aunt Connie smile from her heavenly cloud, where she was probably painting the other angels' portraits.

There was no doubt in her mind that the letter was intended for Constance Greene and not Lila Greene, but she stuck it into her purse anyway and, along with her meager belongings, tossed it in the car.

As she really had no place to go, she decided to leave her fate to chance and flipped a coin. Heads was north, tails south. Tails. After twelve hours of mindless driving, traveling farther and farther away from a life that was lost to her now and impossible to reclaim, she flipped the coin again. Tails. When she saw the highway sign that read *San Diego City Limits,* she suspected her subconscious and the coin were in cahoots.

Chapter Two

IT was the dead of night when Lila pulled into the parking lot of a motel that promised a vacancy. It wasn't until she saw the date written on the form by a bleary-eyed clerk that she realized what day it had just turned: April 1.

"It's April Fools' Day," she told him. He yawned as he ran her charge card through the machine. Lila shrugged and left the office. She took her small suitcase upstairs to her room, closed the door, and sat down on the edge of the mattress.

"What are you doing here?" she asked the reflection in the mirror that hung directly across the room. She saw a small young woman with short black hair and dark eyes, a face heavily shaded by poor overhead lighting and bone-numbing fatigue. She got up and walked over to the mirror, peering at herself, wondering what was so different, and then smiling when she figured out what it was.

Constance Greene had painted Lila often, and, in fact, her likeness was hanging in some of the finer galleries across the nation. That was the way Lila was used to thinking she looked, but the last year or so had taken care of that! She'd seen too much, felt too much, hurt too much. Her eyes reflected it, the lines in her face reflected it, even the new angles brought about by maturity and months of unrelenting grief reflected it.

"Your face has character now," Lila remembered Aunt Connie saying late last fall. "Heaven help me, because I know I'm the one who put it there, but, Lila, how I wish I could paint you now!"

"So do I," Lila whispered, touching the mirror and for one instant seeing Aunt Connie's face in the reflection of her own eyes.

Lila slept dreamlessly and awoke with a start. Sitting in bed as the sun struggled to get through the inadequate drapes, she asked herself exactly what she was doing in San Diego.

"Well, why not San Diego?" she said out loud.

"Because you don't know a soul here," she answered.

"Well, maybe that Yolette woman heard about my genius and actually wants *me* to paint her portrait—"

"Get real. You know she wanted Constance."

"Okay, okay. But I do have to return the check, don't I?"

"There is that."

"And as long as I'm here, maybe I could look for a job. I'm going to need a job, and quickly too, before the MasterCard people find me."

"True—"

"So clam up!"

That issue decided, she quickly showered and dressed, checked out of the motel, and drove to a restaurant. She had enough cash for one scrambled egg and toast, which she ate slowly, with relish. After that, she borrowed the café's map of San Diego and found that to get to Sea Bluff Road, she needed to drive north toward Ocean Beach. She made a few hasty scribbles on a piece of paper so she wouldn't have to try to memorize the way, then walked out into the southern California sunshine.

Three gulls squealed overhead as they flew toward the sea. The street was busy with traffic, while pedestrians dressed in shorts and tank tops sauntered down the sidewalk. From the parking lot, she could see San Diego Bay, a cerulean-blue backdrop for the white triangles of sails and the green headland beyond. The scene made her itch for a paintbrush. Promising herself time to investigate the city of San Diego later, she got in the car and headed north.

A little cottage? Lila asked herself as she drove past one mansion after another. She checked the address Endora Yolette had given her. The house number was 8523, and unless she'd made a mistake, it should be right along—

An oversized mailbox with the right numbers appeared on the left side of the road, which seemed to take an immediate nosedive and disappear down the cliff. Lila made the turn. Iron gates, like the massive jaws of some giant behemoth, stood wide open on either side of the paved driveway. She nosed the car through and began the descent. Learning to drive in San Francisco meant she wasn't intimidated by a little hill or two, and as she drove along the narrow road that twisted its way down toward the sea through a forest of eucalyptus, she fancied she could actually feel a sense of impending adventure flutter in her chest.

Unless Endora had sent the wrong address, her home was not a cottage. What presented itself at the bottom of the sweeping drive was a huge, square white house perched on the edge of the bluff, with an extension off to the side and a red-tile roof. Green lawns and flowering trees and shrubs like the flamboyantly beautiful hibiscus and bougainvillea ringed the yard and the borders.

The showpiece was on the front right side of the house, above a trio of multipaned windows: Showy wisteria draped the front of the house, their long clusters of lavender flowers heavy with perfume. Beneath the windows were lilacs, unexpected this far south and on the coast, their colors ranging from pale to deep purple. Lila switched off the engine and got out of the car, breathing in the heady mixture of flowers and sea, suddenly aware of the sound of the waves as they worked away on the rocks at the base of the cliff.

It was wonderful, she thought. Enchantingly wonderful, she amended as she twirled around to take in the whole effect. The busy road at the top of the drive was completely hidden by the contours of the land and the strategic placement of trees. She reached in the car and grabbed her purse, then almost skipped to the walkway, pausing to admire a planter of marigolds as she climbed the wide brick stairs that led to the arc-shaped front patio.

By the time she knocked on the inset doors, she was dying to see the back of the house. How she was going to wangle an invitation inside when all she really had to do was explain about her aunt's death and return the deposit was still a mystery. Lila's heart leaped as the massive door opened inward and a man in his early thirties looked out.

"Hello," she said. "My name is . . . Miss Greene."

"How did you get down the drive?" he asked pleasantly. He was tall and tanned, dressed casually in baggy beige cotton pants and shirt, sandy-colored hair flopping over his forehead, inviting the speculation that he was a beach lover. He added, "Wasn't the gate closed?"

"No, as a matter of fact, it wasn't," Lila said.

"That's funny." He sidled past Lila and stood on the porch, his hand shading his eyes as he looked toward the circular drive, doing a double take when he saw the beat-up old red car that was the sum of Lila's worldly possessions.

Lila thought she'd like to paint him standing just like that. She made a mental bet with herself that his eyes were chromium oxide green.

"Jay left it open again," he muttered under his breath.

"Excuse me?" Lila asked.

He looked down at her as though he'd temporarily forgotten she was there. "Oh, sorry. Are you here to see Jay? If you are, I'm afraid you're too late."

"No, actually, I'm here to see Endora Yolette."

He frowned. "Is she expecting you?"

"Not exactly—"

"Then I'm afraid I have to tell you my grandmother never sees unscheduled callers."

"How dull for her," Lila said.

"What?"

"Having everything planned like that, I mean. It must be boring."

He raised his sun-bleached eyebrows and regarded her with deep-green eyes. "Don't you know who she is?" he asked.

Lila shrugged. "From what her letter suggests and the bit you've revealed, I'd venture that she's a rather sheltered little old lady."

His bark of laughter startled Lila. " 'Sheltered little old lady,' " he repeated, chuckling. "What's this about a letter?"

Lila stared at him a moment and said, "Look here. I don't know you from Adam, do I? Why should I tell you what your grandmother wrote in private correspondence? If you would just tell her I'm here, mention Miss Greene wants to see her, I'd appreciate it."

He crossed his arms over his chest and stared at her. Finally he said something that sounded like "Just too young," but Lila wasn't really sure, and when she asked him to repeat himself, he only shook his head and said, "Come inside."

The front door was deeply inset into the square of the house, giving a nice overhang outside for protection from the occasional downpour. Lila could see that the glass doors in the back that were opposite the front doors were inset as well so that the middle entry was like a wide tiled hall, an open-looking staircase leading upward on the right side. When the man asked Lila to wait, she crossed to the back of the house and looked out.

What she saw was a huge brick patio furnished with wrought-iron tables and chairs and pottery tubs of brilliant primary-colored flowers. Past the patio was a strip of grass about two hundred feet across, which ended abruptly at the edge of the cliff. Lila looked out to the horizon and saw the long, dark shape of a ship on its way north, maybe heading to San Francisco or across to Hawaii or Japan. For one moment she wished she were aboard the ship, destination unknown, the miles eaten up while she did nothing but stare at the water.

I'd be bored in thirty minutes, she admitted to herself. But maybe if she had her paints and the crew was willing—

"Miss Greene?"

Lila turned to see the man had come back to the entry. He looked very tall from a distance and a lot more substantial than he had when they stood close. He was smiling, almost mischievously, it seemed, and for a moment she wondered if Endora Yolette had forgotten about the letter and had subsequently given this good-looking beach bum permission to throw Lila out of the house. If so, it would appear he found the idea most amusing.

"She'd like to see you," he said. "In here," he added, motioning Lila toward him and the door off to his right.

As she passed him, he said, "I hope you're taking notes, because if you're like the rest of her aspiring flock, you're in for a few surprises."

"What?" Lila asked, totally baffled.

He grinned at her and said, "This way, Miss Greene."

Lila's first impression of the room she now entered was of lilacs. The room faced the front of the house, and the windows had been thrown open so that the lilacs outside almost reached inside, touching the sills in several places, sowing tiny loose flowers like purple snow over the table beneath. Their fragrance was thick in the room, Lila thought, overpowering even the wisteria that competed for window space by daintily dangling down from above. The impression was intensified by the gigantic vase full of still more lilacs that sat upon the desk, by the lavender wallpaper, blue-and-purple swirled rug, overstuffed furniture, and last, but certainly not least, by the woman herself.

She was reclining on a purple sofa, wearing a purple ensemble that seemed to consist of satin pants, kimono, and fuzzy slippers. In point of fact, Lila wasn't sure where the upholstery began and the clothing stopped. Amidst all this purple was a very pale face that showed every one of the eighty-plus years Lila judged it to have lived through, topped with a bubble of silver hair with soft violet highlights. Two blue eyes danced as they appraised Lila, and a bravely painted reddish-purple mouth, the lipstick slightly askew, broke into a wide smile.

"My dear Miss Greene," she said, extending an arm ringed with clattering gold bangle bracelets. "I am Endora Yolette, but, of course, you know that."

Lila was speechless, a fact she could sense was not lost on the man beside her. When she looked at him, he shrugged, his grin still in place. She took a few steps forward and shook the proffered hand.

Endora Yolette used Lila's hand to steady herself as she stood. In that position she didn't seem half as large as she'd first appeared and, in fact, when standing, she lost some of her freakish quality and looked more like an aged version of a child playing dress-up.

She looked at Lila very carefully, and then she said, "You're younger than I thought you'd be!"

"There's a reason for that," Lila said but was cut off short from explaining.

"I suppose there is. But I want to tell you right up front, young woman. I will not pose half naked."

Lila's jaw dropped. She looked at the man and saw his mouth was wide-open too.

"Oh, I know your generation," Endora continued. "So racy. Well, you've read my books, of course, so you know I am an expert on romance, but I will not give in to sensationalism the way some of these modern writers do. Heaving this and pulsating that—

it's disgusting. Romance is in the heart and in the head,'' she added, tapping her own forehead to make her point.

Lila managed to close her mouth and swallow. ''I see—''

''That's good then. Was the deposit enough?''

The man had apparently recovered his wits. ''Deposit? Grandmother, exactly who is this woman?''

''Constance Greene,'' Endora said. ''Oh, I know I didn't tell you I was inviting her to the house, but, Steven, I did so want my portrait done for the drawing room before the party—''

''This isn't Constance Greene,'' he said. He looked at Lila and added, ''You look awfully familiar, but I happen to know Constance Greene is forty-five, and you can't be a day over twenty.''

''Twenty-four—''

''When I was twenty-four—'' Endora began.

''Grandmother, please, let the woman tell us who she really is. I assumed she was one of your worshipers, come to learn about romance writing from the queen herself.''

Endora obviously liked his choice of words. She sat back down on the purple sofa, smoothed out the satin fabric of her kimono with a pair of wrinkled hands, and said, ''Who are you then?''

As Lila told them, she looked more closely at Endora's face. The bones weren't bad, but, of course, the flesh was sagging here and there, though not unpleasantly. The lines and wrinkles in the face were interesting, as was a black beauty mark perched saucily on the right cheekbone. It was difficult to judge the mouth as the lipstick blurred the true shape, but Lila thought that under all the makeup and behind the somewhat outrageous behavior was a brave woman who faced life on her own terms.

As Lila finished explaining, she dug the lavender envelope from her purse and took out the check. "I was down this way," she said lamely, "so I decided to bring the deposit back to you myself."

Steven took the check, looked at it, looked at his grandmother and said, "It's a good thing she didn't try to cash this, Endora. This account was closed six months ago."

"Why wasn't I told?" she snapped.

"You were. You said some of your checks had disappeared and you wanted the account closed just to be sure no one tried to use them."

"That was this account?" she asked, her voice suddenly meek.

"Yes, that was this account."

Endora pouted, which made her purple mouth look like a squashed Red Flame grape. "Well, it doesn't matter, does it, because Constance Greene is dead and can't cash the check. For heaven's sake, dead? At forty-five? That's ridiculous!"

Steven glanced nervously at Lila, and she knew he was worried that Endora's remark might anger or hurt her, but strangely it had just the opposite effect. "I agree wholeheartedly," she said. "I think it's absurd too."

"So, dear, do you paint?"

Lila hadn't realized how much she wanted to hear this question until the words actually left Endora's lips. She nodded her head vigorously and said, "Yes, as a matter of fact, I do. I studied with my aunt for years, and then, of course, I graduated from the university with a degree in art—"

Endora interrupted with a flutter of her hand. "Steven dear, it's almost noon, and we haven't written a word today." She turned her attention to Lila and said, "Then you'll paint my picture?"

"Yes," Lila replied. "I would like to, very much."

"Isn't that grand! And a week or so is enough time?"

"Plenty. Some of the paint may still be wet, but—"

"Lovely, lovely. You watch, Lila. My portrait will be your chance to shine, dear, to show what you can do. It's exactly like one of my books—I believe the sixtieth or so. *Love Under the Bigtop* was the title. The heroine was a circus trapeze artist, but just a backup, you see, and one day the main star sprains her wrist riding a dappled stallion, or rather, falling off a dappled stallion.

"Well, our plucky heroine must take over. After all, the show must go on! So she climbs the ladder, her heart in her mouth, rivulets of fear tingling her spine, and then before she can really think, there comes the trapeze, and she grabs it and swings out high over the main ring below, and then she lets go and flies through the air and for one appalling moment thinks she's misjudged the timing. But just in the nick of time, our hero's strong hands clasp her wrists and—"

"Grandmother," Steven interrupted.

Endora looked at him. "Yes, dear, what is it?"

"Would you like me to write out a new check for Lila's deposit?"

"Didn't I already give her one? Oh, that's right, it was a bad check. Take care of it for me, will you?"

"Gladly."

"And, Lila dear, you watch. You'll be famous!"

"As long as you're pleased with the portrait," Lila said.

"Good. Then that's settled. Steven, get Jay to show Lila to her room, will you? The blue one, dear, because the child is still in mourning." She turned back to Lila and said, "We don't have a black room. Will blue do?"

"Fine," Lila told her, suppressing a smile.

"Jay isn't here," Steven said. "I'll do it myself, though maybe Lila would prefer to stay at a hotel in town and commute—"

"Nonsense!"

"I'd . . . I'd like to stay here," Lila said.

"See? And tell Rose I'd like lunch in here today— alone, I think, so I can muster my creative forces. Shall we work after lunch?"

"If you'd like," Steven said. "If you're feeling up to it."

"Very good, dear. Now run along."

Steven turned to Lila and said, "I guess I'm your host. I'll help you get your things out of the car."

Lila mumbled her thanks. She looked over her shoulder once as she left the room and saw Endora sitting on the sofa, purple on purple on purple.

I'll paint her in red, she thought to herself and was immediately caught up in plotting the portrait.

Chapter Three

"WHAT is all this stuff?" Steven asked as they peered inside the trunk of Lila's car.

"My painting things," she told him. She checked the cardboard box full of paints, solvents, and other paraphernalia to make sure they'd survived the long trip south and found everything in order.

"Then you really can paint?"

Lila turned to face him and said, her voice in a conspiratorial whisper, "No, I can't paint anything more complex than the side of a barn. Don't worry, though. I'll fake it."

"Very funny," he said dryly. "If you had any idea how many people try to take advantage of that old woman in there, you might not be so flip."

His words struck home because she'd said them to herself so many times in the last two years. How many times had aspiring artists knocked on the door and, because they knew Aunt Connie's work, expected her to take time off to listen to their problems and offer solutions? Toward the end Aunt Connie had said, "Turn them away at the door, Lila. I'm afraid I only have enough energy left for myself."

"I was telling the truth about the art degree," Lila said.

He looked unconvinced. Her gaze strayed to the left side of the trunk, to the twenty-four by thirty-six-inch canvas wrapped in a sheet. His gaze followed. "One of yours?" he asked.

All Lila could think of was what Mrs. Row had said the day she and the mister had discussed how they could convert Aunt Connie's perfect studio. "*Who would want to paint someone who looked like that?*" she'd said. Her words had cut Lila to the quick.

"It's one of mine, yes," she said reluctantly.

"May I see it?" he asked, and his voice was amazingly gentle.

Lila knew he had a right to protect his grandmother from charlatans. She lifted the canvas out of the trunk and carefully took off the sheet. "It isn't finished," she explained. "It might never be finished."

He stepped back and looked at the canvas. "Constance Greene," he said.

"Toward the end," she told him.

"She was still beautiful," he said, and when their eyes met, she found nothing but honesty in their depths.

"Yes, she was."

"I read an article on her three years ago," he said

as he helped Lila replace the sheet and put the canvas back in the trunk. "They reproduced a couple of her paintings. One was of a teenage girl sitting amidst the sand dunes. That was you, wasn't it? That's why your face looks familiar."

Lila laughed. "I've changed since then."

"A little," he agreed. "Well, now that I've made a fool of myself, how much of this do you want inside?"

"None of the painting gear until Endora and I have a chance to discuss where she wants her portrait painted. I have a couple of suitcases in the car, though."

So he helped her carry in her suitcases and led the way up the inside stairs to the second floor. The blue room was the third door on the left, facing the ocean. When Endora had called it the blue room, she hadn't been beating around the bush.

"It's a little much," Steven said. "But then again, you're lucky she didn't decide to put you in the green room."

Lila turned away from the window. "Why?"

"Because being in there is like being immersed in split-pea soup. It gives me the creeps."

Lila looked around at the blue curtains, the blue carpet, the blue bedspread, the blue walls—there was even a vase of lilacs, and darned if they didn't look blue too. "I kind of like it," she said. She bent to sniff the lilacs, but these had no aroma whatsoever.

"Well, pardon me for saying so, but it suits you. Are you hungry?"

"As a matter of fact—"

"Lunch in thirty minutes down on the patio." He came to stand beside Lila and look out the window. "Right at that round table down there. With any luck, you'll miss having to meet Cousin Jay over a meal."

Lila looked up into his face. "What does that mean?"

He stared at her for a moment before shaking his head. "Nothing. I shouldn't have said it. Please, make yourself at home. After lunch we'll see what Endora's plans are for you. Until then you're a free woman."

Lila watched him leave, her head full of questions she knew she wouldn't ask and he wouldn't answer even if she did. She sighed heavily, feeling very out of place, very alone. Long an orphan, she was used to being alone, but no matter how far away she'd been before, no matter which school she'd been attending or which study program abroad she'd been involved with, she'd always known Aunt Connie was in California, her anchor, always willing to pull in the chair. The anchor was gone now; Lila was on her own. She knew there was nothing in the world that could change this, but she suspected that knowing something and accepting it were often separate matters.

She spent the next thirty minutes hanging up her clothes, investigating the bedroom and attached bathroom (also blue), and washing up, and promptly at twelve-thirty she made her way downstairs for her first meal at Endora Yolette's house, a big pair of sunglasses resting prominently on the bridge of her nose.

* * *

The table was set for three, but the elusive Jay didn't show up. Steven entertained Lila with stories about his infrequent trips into Mexico. She noticed he didn't talk about his grandmother, nor did he ask her about her aunt. All in all, it was a relief not to have to answer questions, and the thought crossed her mind that he was aware of this and purposely avoided those topics to give her time to assimilate herself into these strange surroundings. If so, she was very thankful, and if so, it meant that Steven Yolette was a very thoughtful man.

The food was served by a woman Steven introduced as Rose. She was tiny, wiry, and somewhat fierce, her hair tied up in a high bun, not one gray strand out of place. "Ms. Endora had fish for lunch," she informed Steven, giving Lila a sidelong look that seemed to say she'd reserve judgment on the newcomer until all the facts were in. "I didn't have any more fish; that's why you're getting yesterday's turkey."

"It's very nice, Rose," Steven said. "Excellent, as a matter of fact. Wouldn't you say so, Lila?"

"Delicious," she agreed quickly.

Rose nodded and disappeared.

Steven, looking after her, said, "Rose has been with Endora for twenty some odd years."

"They are not alike," Lila observed.

"Maybe that's why they're so loyal to each other." He paused and added, "Actually, make no mistake about it. Rose runs the place very efficiently. I'd rather get on Endora's bad side than Rose's!"

After lunch he glanced at his watch. "Endora will still be napping. Would you like to walk around the grounds?"

"I'd love to," Lila said and preceded him down the stairs onto the grass.

They stood on the edge of the bluff for a while, the wind whipping their hair and Lila's cotton skirt. The ocean wasn't as far below as she had expected; by craning her neck, she could just see a sliver of gold sand twinkling in the sunlight.

The beginning of a path to the beach was a few feet farther along the slope, and for a moment Lila was tempted to plunge toward the beach and get her feet wet. The moment passed, and she looked farther along the edge of the grass. A small building that looked very much like a miniature version of the house was nestled in the trees. It looked like a guest house or a camouflaged outbuilding.

Lila took off her glasses and stuck them into the pocket of her skirt, squinting her eyes as she turned her gaze back to the ocean. She loved the feel of the wind and, looking out to sea, felt again that desire to be sailing, aimlessly, away from the land, out toward—

"A penny for your thoughts," Steven said.

Lila looked up at him. "They're not worth a penny."

"Oh, come on now. You're too modest. I'd say from the wistful look on your face and the way your eyes keep straying to the horizon that you wish you were out there, destination unknown, a free soul blowing before the wind. I can see from your startled expression I was close."

"Very close," she admitted.

"That's because I often wish the same thing," he said softly.

She frowned. "Do you?"

He nodded thoughtfully. "I came to visit my grand-mother about a year ago. By chance her secretary had quit the day before, and as she needed a secretary and no one else would put up with her, I sort of filled in. I had just quit my job in advertising to pursue a dream of my own, but her needs distracted me. And then Jay showed up and— Well, there you are."

"And now you wonder if you'll ever get back to your own dream?"

He sighed. "Perceptive as well as beautiful. Well, now you know all about me. What's your story, Lila?"

"It's a pretty ordinary one."

"With Constance Greene as an aunt? That's hard to believe."

Lila smiled. "She was wonderful."

"And you want nothing more than to be just like her?"

Lila looked up at him. "Yes, I suppose you're right. I want to be just like my Aunt Connie. Do you think that's wrong?"

Just then Rose called to them from the patio. "Ms. Endora is awake and calling for you, Steve," she said.

"Saved by the bell," Lila quipped.

As he took her arm, he said, "I think your goal is admirable and very understandable."

"Ah, a diplomat." After a pause she added, "Am I right in assuming Endora is a romance writer?"

"Good heavens, you mean you've really never heard of her?"

Lila shrugged. "I don't read much fiction. My aunt did, but I never looked at the authors' names."

"Well, don't let Endora know, okay? She'd blow a fuse!"

"A purple one," Lila said as they stepped inside. The house seemed dark and welcoming after the bright glare of the outside.

"In case you haven't noticed, ha ha, lilac is Endora's signature color," Steven told her.

"So I suppose she'll want to be painted wearing it?"

"She'll insist." He opened the study door and motioned for Lila to enter first.

Endora was seated at a desk that stood at a right angle to the windows. She looked up as they entered. "Come in, children," she cried. "Wasn't the fish delightful? How Cook does that— Well, you know me, Steven. I can't boil water, as the saying goes."

"You don't need to boil water," he said.

"Is Jay back yet?" she asked, rising to peer through the lilacs toward the front drive.

"Not yet. Endora, you need to talk to Lila about your portrait. I'll get my notes together while you two talk," he added as he walked to a bigger, less grand desk in the far corner that was piled high with papers. Lila couldn't help but notice it was as far removed from the flowery windows as possible. She didn't blame him; left up to her, some serious pruning would be accomplished, and the room would receive a thorough airing as well.

"Of course," Endora said. "Lila, I must be painted in this room, at my desk, pen in hand, a working writer, hard at it on yet another stirring endeavor. Don't you think?"

"I don't know," Lila said. "I work in oils, you know, and they can be quite messy." She looked down at the carpet and added, "Isn't there another room we could use, one with tile floors, perhaps? And perhaps you should be shown relaxing between books, a successful writer at rest?"

Endora screwed up her freshly painted mouth. "I don't know. Steven, what do you think, dear?"

"Leave me out of it," he said from his corner.

Endora spread her hands out on the desk. "I rather pictured myself in front of the lilacs. Aren't they beautiful?"

"Well, yes, they are—"

"Oh, you love them too! I have this special link with the growers, and as these are a hybrid. . . . Oh, I know, I'm rambling on about my precious flowers, but they're gone so quickly, you know. A day or two in the house, and the little flowers turn brown and drop. . . ."

She gestured toward the desk and at the blizzard of dejected flowers that littered the blotter under the vase. "That is why I leave most of them on the bush—they last so much longer."

"That's true," Lila said, thinking to herself that her ability to converse about flowers in general and lilacs in particular was limited.

"Of course, my lilacs don't smell the way they would if we had the cold winters up north."

Lila, whose head was reeling from the suffocatingly sweet fragrance of the flowers, said, "Really?"

"That's why I use this," Endora said, opening her file cabinet and producing a can of lilac-scented air freshener.

"You're not going to spray that stuff while I'm in here," Steven said firmly.

"No, dear, of course not." Endora dropped the can back into the file drawer and closed it with a nudge from her hip.

Lila could see that they would go on talking about lilacs forever if she didn't gain control of the direction of the conversation. "How about this?" she proposed. "We'll pick a rather grand chair—I think I saw one in the front entry that would suit you well—and we'll put it in front of a nondescript background that won't compete with your face for attention. Then on a table by your side, we'll put a huge vase of freshly picked lilacs. Maybe you could hold one of your books, or it could be on the table beside the lilacs, if you'd like. And as for your clothes, choose something your friends and family will recognize, something that suits you."

"Something lavender, of course," Endora said firmly.

"Okay," Lila said. She'd known all along that red was out, but it had been a nice thought while it lasted.

"Then we must find a room that suits me . . . and you," Endora said. She swept past Lila and out the door. Lila looked toward Steven, but he was engrossed in the papers spread out before him on the desk, seemingly oblivious to everything around him. Lila followed Endora out into the entry.

Endora threw open the door opposite her own. This room was furnished with tapestry-covered cherrywood furniture, all very exquisite and predominately—what else? Lila thought—purple. A small unused fireplace occupied one corner. The front windows were open in this room too, but there were no lilacs to brush against the sill and perfume the still, warm air. One large wall was painted a light lavender color, and the rugs on the floor were expensive-looking throw rugs.

"The lighting in here is very nice," Lila noted.

"That's where my portrait is going to hang," Endora said, motioning toward the blank wall. "Everyone will see it the minute they come into the room, and, of course, once it's hung, I'll take special care to make sure the doors are left open all the time."

"I think this would make a fine place to paint it," Lila told her. "We can roll back that carpet, and I have a mat I can put down over the tiles."

"If you'd like," Endora said. "How big will it be?"

"Any size you'd like."

"I have lovely hands," Endora said immodestly, holding her hands out in front of her—admiring, Lila supposed, the three amethyst rings that sparkled amid fields of diamonds. "I would like them to be included."

"Okay. I stretch my own canvas. Judging by the expanse of that wall, I'd say something rather large."

"Yes, yes. I love it! Something large and grand."

Lila smiled. Endora went back to her study, saying something about how she just had to get to work on her latest book, and Lila began setting the stage.

She rolled the carpet back, then hauled the wicker chair in from the front hall and set it before the wall. It was going to be awkward, painting Endora sitting in the chair, because her face would be so much lower than Lila's eyes. For a moment Lila thought longingly of Aunt Connie's model's stand, hacked apart the day before yesterday and no doubt hauled to the dump by now.

She turned away from the chair and looked for a small table that would look good with it. Toward this end, she wandered through the house, running into a solemn young woman in the dining room. The woman wore a faded yellow shirt and blue jeans, and when Lila spoke to her, she answered in monosyllables while staring at her shoes. After a slightly difficult-to-understand conversation, Lila discovered that the woman, whose name was either Fay or Rae, was employed by Endora as a "twice-a-week maid."

Lila left her to finish mopping the tile floor and poked her nose into what turned out to be the kitchen. The cook looked up from his stove and waved a spoon at Lila, inviting her to come taste the tomato-clam soup. She declined with a smile and continued her search, but she found no suitable table until she remembered the nightstand in her room, or, as Endora insisted on calling it, the blue room. She ran upstairs, took the lamp, clock, and her own purse off the small glass-topped table, dragged it out into the middle of the room, and regarded it with a critical eye.

The table was heavy, but step by step she got it downstairs and into what Endora had called the sitting room. It looked perfect next to the airy wicker. A vase of lilacs just happened to be on the coffee table, and Lila moved them to the glass-topped table. They were silk lilacs, she noticed, but for now would do quite nicely. She'd darken the background, she thought, but nothing further could be accomplished until she discovered what Endora chose to wear. That much done, she went out to her car and began lugging in the paints, the easel, and all the other supplies she'd brought with her from San Francisco.

"I shall sit for you tomorrow morning," Endora announced that night over soup. She'd changed into a gaudy sweatshirt embroidered with faux jewels, metallic thread, and large pink pearls, all on a lilac background. This outfit suggested to Lila that Endora didn't own a piece of clothing that wasn't some shade of purple.

"I'd rather spend tomorrow sketching you," Lila said. "Informal sketches, perhaps, while you work?"

Endora looked at Steven, who shrugged goodnaturedly. She turned her attention back to Lila and said, "You're the expert, dear. Hasn't Cook done a wonderful job with this soup?"

"Delicious," Lila said, wishing it didn't taste so strongly of clams.

While Steven and Endora talked about Endora's

book, Lila stared at the chair, where she presumed Jay was supposed to be sitting. They were seated inside at a white French Provincial table, and his place had been set as at lunch. Lila couldn't help but be curious about this man she'd heard mentioned so many times but had never met, and she wondered if he could possibly live up to the image she was building of him in her mind.

"Lila dear, I said, do you like my china?"

Lila looked at Endora. "I'm sorry. I guess I was daydreaming. Yes, yes, the china is lovely."

"It's bone china," Endora informed her. "I had it made specifically for me. The flowers are lilacs, can you tell?"

Lila peered through the thick red soup. "Oh, yes, aren't they exquisite?"

She looked up in time to see Steven fold his napkin over his mouth, but the dancing lights in his eyes made it very obvious he was laughing.

"I adore lilacs," Endora said as Rose took away the soup bowls. "They're my signature flower. You've no doubt read my first book, *The Lilac Heart*?"

Looking for a way to dodge a flat out "No, I haven't read that or any other of your books," Lila said, "When was it written?"

Endora tapped her lip with her fingernail. "Let's see. That would have been written in 1938, wouldn't it, Steven?"

"I wouldn't know, Grandmother," he said as Rose delivered beef Stroganoff to the table.

"Yes, it was 1938."

"A little before Lila's time," Steven said dryly.

"Nonsense. My books are classics."

"If you have a copy, I'd love to borrow it tonight," Lila said.

Endora beamed. "Of course. In my study, on the bookcase behind the desk. All two hundred and fifteen books are there, aren't they, Steven?"

"Unless someone sneaked into the house and stole them," he said with a grin.

"You tease. Anyway, what I was going to say is that the public adored that first book, and ever after I have worked lilacs into each and every one of my projects."

"Over two hundred of them," Lila said. "You must be running out of ways to do it."

"No, no, no, my dear. On the contrary. What was it last time, Steven?"

He looked up, a loaded fork halfway to his mouth. "It was, and I quote, 'Jessie lifted the .357 Magnum. The moment before she fired it, she thought to herself how ironic it was that the neon light flashing outside the window made the gun barrel look a fragile shade of purple, almost lilac, the color of the ocean near sunset.'"

"Yes, that's right." Endora bit at her lower lip and added, "That was my idea?" It looked to Lila as though she were troubled by something.

"Of course," he said and took a bite of noodles. After he swallowed, he patted his grandmother's hand and added, "Grandma, why don't you eat your dinner before it gets cold? Cook will be furious with you if you waste his efforts."

"Of course," she said, and the concerned look fled her eyes. It returned a moment later when she looked at the empty chair beside Lila. "Steven, hasn't Jay come home yet?"

He took a sip of water. "I haven't seen him."

"Where was he going?" she asked.

"He said something about the marina."

"Your boat, dear?"

"I hope not."

"Steven!"

They exchanged long looks; then Endora seemed to remember Lila. "What you must think of us, talking about people you don't know. Or did you meet Jay this morning?"

"No, he was already gone," Lila said.

"Hm—well, I suppose you'll fall head over heels in love with him," Endora said as she buttered a roll. "All the girls do, don't they, Steven?"

Lila looked up at Steven. He was staring at her, and she lowered her eyes right away.

Endora said, "Don't they?"

"Most of them," Steven answered.

"He's a good-looking boy, that grandson of mine," Endora said as she took a bite of her roll and tackled her dinner. Lila knew from the way she said it that she wasn't referring to Steven, and she chanced another look at him, curious as to how he was taking this, but his attention was focused over her shoulder. As Lila began to turn, Endora looked up from her plate.

"Jay darling," she cried. "Come in, dear, you're late!"

Chapter Four

THE first thing Lila noticed about Jay Yolette was the color of his eyes, an ultramarine blue, the same color as his shirt. They were heavily lashed, supremely confident, and he used them to glance first at his grandmother, then his cousin, and lastly, provokingly, at Lila.

The second thing she noticed was his mouth, composed of two almost perfect lips, the bottom just a tad fuller than the top. His mouth was mobile, reflecting in an instant chagrin at being late, surprise upon seeing Lila, and then, along with his eyes, speculation that made Lila look quickly down at her dinner.

"I left word with Steve that I wouldn't be back until after dinner, didn't I, Steve?"

Before Steven could answer, Jay was beside Lila.

"Of course, at the time I had no idea this lovely creature would be present, or I would have hurried back."

"You didn't tell me when you'd be back," Steven said, glancing at Lila.

"Come sit down," Endora entreated. "Sit there by Lila. It's so exciting, dear, because she's quite a famous portrait painter, and she's consented to paint me!"

"Famous is she, as well as gorgeous?" Jay said as he sat down in the chair next to Lila.

"I'm not famous," Lila said softly.

"Of course you are," Endora insisted. "I abhor false modesty, dear. Your paintings are hanging in all the galleries. Why, even Steven—"

"Grandmother," Steven interrupted, "Lila is Constance Greene's niece, remember?"

Endora batted her eyelashes a couple of times and then laughed. "Yes, of course. What am I thinking of? Constance Greene died."

Lila nodded. It was kind of like desensitizing training, she reflected wryly. Two days ago the thought of Aunt Connie actually having died was enough to startle her anew and plunge her into despair, but Endora Yolette said it so matter-of-factly, and so often, that it was beginning to sink in, the blunt words forming some kind of protective overcoat from the pain.

Steven spared Lila another agonized look, and she decided she'd have to tell him how his grandmother was helping her, in a way, to cope with her loss.

Jay put his hand on Lila's arm. "I'm sorry about

your aunt, but delighted you're here," he said. Up close, he seemed a little older than he had from the doorway. There were fine lines at the corners of his eyes and a lived-in look to the set of his mouth. Instead of his being younger than Steven, she began to suspect he might be a year or two older.

"Ring the bell there and call Rose," Endora said, "and have something to eat, dear. You must be famished."

Jay poured himself a glass of red wine and sat back in his chair, a man who could, in his black slacks and linen jacket, look elegant and casual at the same time. "Not really," he said. "I ate in town."

Steven looked up, but he didn't say anything. Jay must have noticed the quick glance, however, and said, "No, not on your boat, Steve. I told you I'd steer clear of it, and I have. I was an invited guest on the Ransoms' yacht."

"General Ransom, that old billy goat!" Endora squealed. She leaned toward Lila and added, "He pinched me once, right on my fanny!"

Steven smiled, Jay howled, and Lila said, "Did he really?"

"Yes, dear, and none too gently, either."

"And what did you do?" Lila asked.

"She hauled off and decked him," Steven said serenely.

Endora nodded. "That's right." She ate a strip of beef, then waved her empty fork at Jay. "So, darling, tell us what you did aboard the Ransoms' yacht."

''He probably romanced Donna, the general's nubile daughter,'' Steven said.

Jay laughed. ''Indeed I did, or at least I tried. It's not that Donna wasn't willing, but good old Daddy seems to have his heart set on the strong, silent type like Steve. However, as Donna can't hold a candle to Lila, I find condolence on my own doorstep.''

Lila laughed, but she found her gaze straying to Steven, who seemed to be ignoring his cousin's teasing and concentrating on his dinner. Jay put his arm along the back of Lila's chair. His fingers touched her bare arm in a friendly manner. She turned to face him and was almost bowled over by the blue of his eyes. His face was almost perfect, saved from being pretty by a strong nose and jawline. Besides his startling good looks, he had a quality Aunt Connie used to refer to as ''animal magnetism,'' a quality that made Lila feel uneasy and attracted in the same breath.

He ran his hand through his perfectly cut dark hair and said, ''You're almost finished eating. How about a walk in the moonlight?''

Lila swallowed. She looked across the table at Steven, who was paying a lot of attention to folding his napkin. She said, ''That's a great idea. Would anyone like to join us?''

''Oh, not me,'' Endora insisted. ''It's way past my bedtime. Lila, I've been thinking about my books. Start with the first one and work your way through the entire collection. I really must insist you read several before you portray me on canvas. I know, as a fellow artist, you'll understand.''

Lila, wondering how anyone could be expected to read over two hundred books inside a week, said, "Of course." She looked at Steven and added, "How about you? Doesn't a nice walk sound good?"

He looked up quickly. "Not me, no thanks. I have the notes from today to look over."

Jay stood up and touched Lila's shoulder. "We won't walk far," he promised. "If my attentions alarm you, you can scream, and Cousin Steve and good old Rose will run to your rescue. Let's go."

With a last look toward Steven, Lila rose and was instantly guided out the door and away into the darkness.

"The moon makes a path across the water," Lila said. "It almost seems as though you could walk across the path, doesn't it?"

Jay put his arm around Lila and spoke into her hair. "Anything seems possible out here in the moonlight with you and the breeze—"

Lila ducked out from beneath his arm. "It's a warm wind," she said. "Listen to the way it rustles the leaves."

They were standing on the bluff, down the slope from where Lila and Steven had talked earlier in the day, nearer the stand of tall eucalyptus trees. They'd reached this spot after walking all the way around the well-tended grounds. Lila found her attention wandering to the small building she'd noticed earlier. The lights were on now, though the drapes were closed, and Lila thought it looked enchanting in among the trees.

"Come here," Jay urged, his hand finding Lila's arm, coaxing her back to his side.

She politely but firmly moved his hand. "Please, Jay. I love the smell of eucalyptus, don't you?"

He put his hands on her shoulders, and she felt his warm breath near her forehead. "I love the smell of you," he said.

"Jay, honestly," she said as she ducked out from beneath his hands before his lips connected with her forehead. "Knock it off, will you? I feel like I used to feel in college when I found myself on a blind date with a guy who was all hands."

He laughed, but one hand stayed on her arm and the other stole around her waist. She gently elbowed his stomach and pulled away again.

"Don't you listen?" she asked.

He looked down at her, his face little more than shadows. "As a matter of fact, I do listen, Lila. I listen to the way your voice sounds, not just the words you say."

"I see," she said. "My mouth is saying no, no, no while my eyes are saying yes, yes, yes?"

"Since it's too dark to see your eyes clearly, I'm paying attention to the tone of your voice. Come here. One little kiss—"

Lila started laughing. "You're too much," she said at last. "You're so smooth, you've forgotten what it's like to be around a woman who doesn't swarm all over you like a tropical vine."

"Lila—"

"No, listen. And listen to my words and don't try to read anything into the inflection of my voice. When I tell a guy to back off, I expect him to back off, is that clear?"

"Lila—"

"I'm not playing hard to get. I don't know you from Adam, and contrary to what you're apparently accustomed to, I don't go around kissing strangers."

This time he laughed. "Okay."

"Okay?"

"You win. I'll keep my hands to myself."

Lila smiled. "Good. I'm sorry if I offended you—"

"Now, don't ruin the effect of your fire-and-brimstone speech by apologizing when you know it's me who owes you the apology—which is hereby given."

"Okay."

They stood in silence for a while until Jay said, "He's at it again."

"Who's at what?" Lila asked.

"Cousin Steve. Burning the midnight oil, or whatever it is people burn nowadays." He sat down on the grass and tugged on the hem of Lila's slacks. "Sit down. I promise I won't touch you."

Lila sat down beside him and looked toward the big house. She had no idea which was Steven's room, but as all the second-story lights seemed to be out, she wasn't sure what Jay was talking about. Thanks to the full moon, Jay must have been able to see which direction she looked, for he added, "Not the house. Steve has a workshop separate from the main place. Over there.''

Lila's gaze followed the direction Jay pointed and saw the small building. ''That's where Steven works?''

''Yep. Keeps it locked tighter than a drum too.'' He lay back on the grass. ''Come on, get comfortable, pretty Lila. I promised, remember?''

''I am comfortable, thanks,'' she said, staring at the building.

''Don't you trust me?''

She looked down at him. ''No. I don't believe I do.''

''Now I'm hurt.''

''I'll bet.''

''Come on. Lie back here and look at the stars.''

Lila sighed and lay back on the grass. The full moon faded the night sky, but a few stars were visible, and she gazed until she found a few favorite constellations.

''So, you're a painter,'' Jay said.

''I'm a painter.''

''Aren't you kind of young?''

''I'm twenty-four,'' she informed him and then told him about her aunt.

''So my wacky grandmother hired your aunt to paint her portrait, and you showed up instead?''

Lila propped her head on her elbow and looked at Jay. ''That's right.''

''How much is she paying you?''

Lila sat up. ''I really don't think that's any of your business,'' she snapped.

''Don't get huffy on me. I was just hoping she was

paying you enough. Steve can be kind of tight on the old pocket strings.''

''This has nothing to do with Steven,'' she said.

''Don't kid yourself. He controls Endora and her money.''

''He seems to be very kind to her and very concerned about her welfare.''

''It suits him,'' Jay said softly.

To change the subject, she said, ''You live here full-time? What do you do?''

He laughed softly. ''As in for a living? Well, I dropped out of college after a couple of years, and until recently I was in retail sales. Right now I'm between jobs, just paying Grandmother a visit. She's going to be eighty-six in a few days,'' he added.

''I know. That's why she commissioned me to paint her portrait.''

''How do you go about that?'' he asked.

''What do you mean?''

''I mean, the woman is old and vain. How do you make her look like she wants to look without compromising your art?''

''Endora is a very vibrant, unique-looking woman,'' Lila said. ''I'll paint what I see. She'll like it.''

He laughed again. ''Your confidence unnerves me, Lila Greene.''

Lila was feeling the effects of a long day—and a trying conversation, for she didn't feel at all confident. She yawned. ''I'm tired,'' she said as she stood. ''Are you coming in now?''

He rose gracefully to his feet. "No fun staying out here alone now, is there?"

The door to the study was at a right angle to the foot of the stairs. Lila saw that Endora had politely left it ajar with the lights on, no doubt so Lila would remember to take an armload of books up to her room. She paused at the door and said, "Thanks, Jay, for the walk, and . . . everything." She pushed open the door and was instantly assaulted by the perfume of the lilac air freshener that had permeated the closed room. Jay touched her shoulder and gently turned her around.

He leaned down and kissed her cheek, as close to her mouth as possible, and though she supposed the kiss was meant to be friendly, he was too skilled and too handsome for there not to be some effect.

"Now don't say a word," he said softly. "I know what I said, and I mean to stick to it. Good night."

Lila put her fingers to her lips, knowing darn good and well that the kiss meant he had no intentions of sticking to anything. She turned on her heels and entered the study as Jay's footsteps ascended the stairs.

Endora's bookcase was against the wall behind her desk. Row upon row of paperback books were crowded into the narrow space. Lila leaned down to scan the titles, straightening abruptly when she heard a discreet cough. She twirled around, and there, standing over his own desk in the far corner, was Steven.

From his vantage point she knew that he'd seen the kiss and, also from his vantage point, that it would have appeared to be more than it was. She said, "That little cough would have been more polite if you'd come up with it a couple of minutes earlier.''

"Excuse me," he said. "I didn't expect you and Jay to carry on right here in the room.''

"We were not carrying on!" she said indignantly.

He shrugged. "I remembered your deposit a few minutes ago and came back to write a check. Didn't you think there might be someone else in the room when you saw the lights were on?''

"I thought Endora left them on for me," she said.

"Well, she didn't.''

She nodded. "Okay, you saw what you saw. It was nothing, believe me." She turned back to the books and took two from either end of the collection. She walked to the door, pausing when Steven called out to her.

"What?" she said.

He crossed the room. "Your deposit, remember?"

Lila took the check and, without looking at it, slipped it into her pocket. "Thank you."

"Before you go, were you aware you have a eucalyptus leaf in your hair, there in the back?"

Lila felt the back of her head with her hand. Sure enough, she felt the long dry leaf entangled in her black strands. She said, "Thank you," and exited out of the room and up the stairs, her cheeks flaming for no good reason.

Chapter Five

Iᴛ took a while to get the leaf out of her hair, and Lila knew, she *knew,* Steven thought she'd gotten it when she rolled around in the grass with Jay. She didn't know why it bothered her so much that he should think that—after all, she'd only met him a few hours earlier—but it did. She also knew there was no way to explain things without giving him the impression that his opinion was important to her; she repeatedly told herself she didn't give a hoot what he thought about her. It was none of his business. Besides, if he was so quick to make judgments, she really didn't care to talk with him again.

In the back of her mind, she knew all this was foolishness. All he'd done was point out a leaf. Everything else was in her own mind.

She felt restless. She changed into a nightgown, but

though she got under the thin blanket, she knew she wasn't going to be sleeping anytime soon. She was embarrassed about the stupid leaf, confused about Jay, annoyed with Steven, and worried about her ability to paint Endora's portrait satisfactorily. Was Endora as vain as Jay insinuated she was? What would Aunt Connie have done?

One of Aunt Connie's pieces of sage advice had been, ''Put your emotions to work for you.'' Lila got up and fetched the sketchbook and a charcoal pencil from her case. For the next hour, she made quick, sure lines, creating all the people she'd met that day, from the twice-a-week maid to the cook stirring his soup. She sketched Jay looking down at her, his expression sensual and exciting; Endora emerged amid the lilacs, like an antique sprite; Steven stood on the bluff, one hand shading his eyes as he looked off toward the horizon. Lila eventually fell asleep with her sketches cluttering the bedspread and the floor, the charcoal pencil gripped loosely in her right hand, Steven's face staring out to sea.

''What do you think, dear?''

Lila didn't know what to think, let alone say. Endora had come down to work in a lavender-colored silk wrapper with marabou trim. The outfit was so outrageous, Lila was inclined to smile. She glanced at Steven, who warned her from this course of action with a barely perceptible shake of his head.

''I think it's too fancy for the portrait,'' Lila said at last.

"Really? Maybe you're right."

"Do you have something with a simple neckline?"

"Of course."

"Then try that."

"After lunch," she said and sat down behind her desk.

Lila perched on the sofa, sketchbook at hand. She made a few preliminary sketches, most of her attention directed toward her work, while Endora dictated her next book to Steven.

"Back to *Call of the Wind*," she said. "Let's see: And then the girl, what's her name—"

"Desdemona, Grandmother."

"Yes, that's right. Okay, start when she comes into the room after that party."

"You mean the funeral?"

"Yes, yes, the funeral," Endora said. She sat up straighter, and when she spoke again, her voice was softer, younger. "Desdemona tossed her mane of corn-silk hair defiantly," Endora dictated. "'I will not marry you, Mr. Smythe, and that's final,' she said, her cornflower-blue eyes filling with tears when she thought of what her poor papa, fresh in his grave, would think of her. But life was for the living, and she couldn't sacrifice her own happiness for anyone, not even for the memory of the dear man who had raised her, not when she truly loved the cavalier Robert Turnstone." Endora, tapping her finger against her right cheek, said, "Did you get all that, Steven?"

"Every word," he said.

Lila ripped off a sheet of paper, let it fall to the

floor, and immediately began another drawing. When Endora dictated, she assumed a different look, and Lila was determined to capture it.

" 'But you have no means of support,' Mr. Smythe retorted hotly, 'and your father promised me your hand.'

"Desdemona looked up, her eyes blazing. 'I begin to see, sir,' she said, 'that you're after more than a wife. You're after my papa's land!'

"Mr. Smythe laughed. 'You will be mine, Desdemona, you will be mine. There's really nothing you can do about it, my dear.'

"Desdemona looked longingly through the big eastern-facing window. The day had grown stormy, the trees bent with the wind. When would Robert Turnstone come to her aid? Would he be in time?"

Lila knew she'd captured what she wanted when she glanced from the paper to the living model and for one microsecond was unsure which was which. She added a few lines to represent shadows, wrinkles, and contouring. She knew now how she'd pose Endora—straight on, no compromise, eyes snapping, hands crossed in lap, chin slightly uplifted, purple mouth in a knowing smile that bordered on a grin. It would be a tad impertinent, she thought, just like the woman herself.

In the back of her mind, she heard Endora's voice unwind the story of the beautiful Desdemona, the conniving Mr. Smythe, and the dashing Robert Turnstone. She paid no attention to the actual words as she did a charcoal study of Endora's eyes and several of her mouth. She found the beauty spot was lower on the cheek, more toward the mouth, than she'd remembered it being, and added it to each drawing. She decided when it came time to paint, she'd tone down the lipstick.

Gradually Lila became aware that Endora had stopped speaking. Lila looked up to see Steven standing over the drawings she'd thrown to the floor in her haste. "Interesting," he said.

Lila quickly gathered her drawings together as though she were a mother duck corralling her ducklings, which she supposed, following her metaphor, made Steven a hungry sea gull.

"I didn't mean to pry," he said, stepping away.

Lila nodded. "I know. I guess I'm just a little unsure of myself."

Glancing at the top drawing, he said, "I can't imagine what you feel you have to be unsure about."

"Thank you, Steven."

He stared at her for a long moment; then they both looked away at once. Steven moved back to his desk while Lila stood and stretched.

"I'm famished," Endora announced. "A long morning spent in honest pursuit of creative truth does that, don't you think, Lila?"

"Yes," Lila agreed, deciding that she agreed with the essence of the statement even if the wording was a trifle confusing.

"Steven, be a lamb and tell Rose to serve me in here again. I'm too creatively exhausted to make small talk over lunch." Endora put the back of her hand against her forehead and reclined theatrically on the lush purple sofa. Lila made a very quick, very simple line drawing of the pose.

"Okay," Steven said.

"Lila, I see you drawing away like a woman possessed. Are you going to show me what you have?"

"Not yet," Lila told her, shuffling the new drawing into the stack.

"I want to see," she said, pouting.

"Think of it like a first draft," Lila suggested. "I'd like to edit it a bit before showing it to you."

Put in familiar terms, Endora said she understood. She asked Lila how she was coming with the books, and Lila assured her she was coming along fine, though the truth of the matter was that she'd been too upset the night before to so much as open a cover. She decided to spend the hour after lunch reading.

She ran upstairs before lunch, opened the window in the blue room for ventilation, and spread the drawings out on the floor. One by one she quickly sprayed them with fixative.

Jay was absent again—gone into town, Steven explained as though Lila would want to know, which she didn't, to be fitted for a tuxedo. He didn't explain why Jay would need a tuxedo, and Lila didn't ask.

They ate at the patio table again, under an umbrella whose fringe danced in the wind. It was a particularly warm day, and Lila welcomed the feel of the sun creeping into her bones. She almost fell asleep waiting for Rose to deliver sandwiches, then ate lightly, noticing Steven didn't eat much, either.

After lunch Steven said, "I don't know about you, but I could use some exercise. Let's go down to the beach."

Lila started to say yes, then remembered her reading assignment. "I can't," she told him.

"I saw how excited you looked for a moment; then your expression went cold, just like that," he said, snapping his fingers to illustrate his point. "I'm sorry about last night. I really didn't mean to sneak around or spy on you and Jay—"

"It's not that," Lila assured him, embarrassed to the point of potential spontaneous combustion.

"Of course it is. I sounded . . . well, let's just say I realize I sounded gruff."

"Gruff?"

He grinned. "Grouchy, snoopy, I don't know. But what you do while you're here is your business. You wouldn't be the first woman to become . . . infatuated . . . with Jay."

Lila laughed. "Sounds like sour grapes to me," she quipped. "Did he steal away your own true love?"

"Hardly!" He looked at Lila's smiling mouth and added, "Okay, I deserved that. Sometimes when I talk about Jay, I sound jealous, don't I? Our fathers were close, you know, and as kids so were we. The truth of the matter is that I am jealous of Jay, but not the way you think. Have you noticed that the more I explain, the deeper I wedge my foot into my mouth?"

"Now that you mention it," Lila said. "And as much as I'm enjoying it, I hate to disappoint you with the truth, which is that I haven't read even one of your grandmother's books. Before I goof off, I have to at least look through a couple.''

He considered her for a second and said, ''Oh, I wouldn't do that.''

''But I would. It seems important to her.''

He shook his head. ''If you feel you really must, read the early ones. They're the ones she likes to discuss.''

''Not her recent work?''

He cleared his throat. ''No. Listen, play hooky. You agreed to paint the woman, not research her. Endora can, at times, be a little demanding.''

''No kidding,'' Lila said, laughing.

Steven stood. ''Are you coming down to the beach with me?''

She looked up at him. ''You swift talker, you. Okay, let me go put away my drawings and put on a bathing suit.''

''I'll meet you back here in fifteen minutes.''

Fifteen minutes later they started down the path that twisted its way to the small beach below. Steven went first, reaching back on occasion to grasp Lila's hand and steady her when the slope was tricky. Toward the end, the path merged into the rocks, and they jumped the last three feet to the beach.

Lila kicked off her tennis shoes and dug her toes into the warm sand. She pulled off her long T-shirt and felt the sun hit the white untanned skin of her back and stomach.

''You're going to burn to a crisp,'' Steven said. He'd pulled off his shirt and was dressed in a pair of baggy swim trunks. Lila was reminded of the first impression she'd had of him—a beach bum, a surfer, a sun worshiper. She realized she was staring at the muscles in his broad shoulders and looked out toward the waves. But the thought ran across her mind that here was a man with an extremely good-looking body and a personality to match!

The beach was situated in a small cove, cut off at high tide from the north and the south by large rocks. It was private and captivating. Lila ran toward the water, aching to get wet.

It was colder than she'd thought it was going to be, and she squealed in icy delight as the water swished up around her knees. Steven charged past her and dove under a wave, emerging a moment later a few feet farther out than Lila.

"The bottom slopes pretty fast," he warned. "It's not a great swimming beach. In fact, I wouldn't go out much farther than this."

Lila took another step forward as a wave retreated. Sandy water swirled around her legs. Another wave broke a couple of feet in front of her, and she held her nose and pushed her way through the foaming white water.

"Yikes! It's cold!" she screamed.

Steven dove under the water again, and when Lila wasn't struggling to keep from being swept out to sea, she was enchanted with his brown shape darting this way and that, the look of the sun as it kissed the golden highlights in his sandy hair, the green of his eyes that was an exact match to the ocean. He wasn't as beautiful as Jay, but she found him infinitely more attractive, and suddenly she knew that she wanted to paint him surrounded by water, which seemed his natural environment.

With her teeth clattering, Lila made her way out of the sea and collapsed on the warm sand. Her skin looked a little blue, she thought, and though she knew she should cover up almost at once, it was too tempting to lie back and let the sun undo the cold.

She felt a shadow over her face and opened her eyes. Steven was standing over her. He held her T-shirt in his hands. She sat up and took the shirt while he flopped down beside her.

She put the shirt on and shook out her short straight hair.

"You look like a seal," he said.

"Oh, thank you," she said with a laugh. "A rather washed-out one, wouldn't you say?"

"A very pretty seal with pink skin."

"I thought the same of you while you were swimming," Lila said cautiously. "Not the pink part, mind you, the seal part. You're very at home in the water, aren't you?"

He looked at her, then away. "Yes," he said simply.

"Why does that observation bother you?"

Steven sighed and rubbed the back of his neck with a tanned hand. "It shouldn't, should it?"

"But it does?"

"I guess so. It's all part of that abandoned dream I told you about."

She waited for him to explain, but he clearly didn't

want to. "I know something about abandoned dreams," she told him.

He stretched out on the sand, his hands crossed under his head, and said, "Tell me."

"You first," she said.

He looked right into her eyes. "Please, Lila. As fascinated as I am with you, I'm that bored with my own little tale of woe. Tell me about your dreams."

"Are you sure?"

"Positive. Start with what you want out of life."

"That's easy. All I've ever wanted to do is paint," she said softly, her gaze directed at the waves as they hissed and foamed upon the sand. "It's a competitive, exacting skill, believe it or not, and there are more critics than there are artists, and they're not known for showing mercy. I can still remember the day I graduated. I was scared witless."

"Scared?" he asked. "You don't strike me as the kind of woman to be afraid of her future."

"But I was. I had a couple of job offers, and they were good ones if you're talking money, which I wasn't that keen on. I was going to take the one in Houston, and then Aunt Connie showed up for the graduation ceremony. I knew the first second I saw her that something was dreadfully wrong with her. She'd lost weight, and her skin looked funny, but more than that, there was something about her eyes."

"You didn't know she had cancer until then?" Steven asked.

Without looking at him, she answered, "She kept it from me. She told me she was too busy to visit the campus. I was so wrapped up in things at school, I didn't push the point. And then she came to graduation, and I found out the truth.''

"And you went back home with her instead of taking the job in Houston?''

"She told me not to,'' Lila said, heedless of the tears that rolled down her cheeks. "She told me she could hire someone, but, Steven, the thought of a stranger sharing her last two years was more than I could take. At least, that's what I told myself.''

Steven was silent while Lila wiped her face dry with her arm. After several minutes he said, "So you wonder if you used your aunt's illness as an excuse to hide from the real world because you lacked faith in your talent?''

She looked swiftly at him. "I guess I do,'' she said at last.

He was silent again. Lila heard the gulls squawking overhead and for a second wished she were aloft with them, riding the warm currents, her concerns no deeper than the acquisition of her next meal.

"What did your aunt have to say about your ability?'' he asked.

"She was my aunt,'' Lila said. "What was she supposed to say?''

"From what I've read about her, the truth,'' Steven said succinctly. "Did she ever have you help her with her work?''

Lila told him about the portraits for the bank, about how, at her aunt's request, she'd painted the last two to complete the series.

"There you go. Would she have let you finish a commission if she didn't trust your talent?"

"I don't know—"

"Yes, you do. You knew her better than anyone, right? Wasn't she a perfectionist?"

"Yes, but she was also very sick."

"I didn't know her, of course," Steven said, "but I somehow think she would have found a way to honor her commitments herself if she hadn't had you to rely on. And while I'm no expert, judging from the tiny bit of your work I've seen, I'd bet a bundle you have a deep, abiding talent and, in your heart, you know it."

Lila rested her cheek on her bent knee and looked down at him. "Makes me sound a bit vain, doesn't it?" she asked.

"I don't think an artist, any artist, can have the heart to create without believing in himself. No, I don't think it's vanity; I think it's faith."

She smiled. "Well, it sounds better, anyway."

"May I ask you a question?" he asked, sitting up.

"Sure."

"Why did you come all the way here from Frisco so soon after your aunt's death? I wouldn't ask except that you couldn't have known if Endora would accept you as a substitute for Constance Greene or give you the boot. That and you looked a little defiant and a little lost when you showed up."

"Did I?" She told him about the bills and selling the house, actually making it through the story without a new onslaught of tears. When she'd finished, she sighed heavily.

"And you wonder about your motives in caring for your aunt," he asked, "when as soon as the need and the opportunity arose, you struck out on your own? Maybe you underestimate yourself."

"Maybe I do, but who doesn't?" Lila asked.

"Cousin Jay," Steven said and laughed. He grew serious again almost at once and put his hand on Lila's arm. "The past is over, part of history now, a foundation, isn't it? What matters to you, as an artist, is the future. You're right on the threshold, with two years of maturity and your aunt's legacy of talent and skill to sustain you."

"Right on the threshold," Lila repeated. "Yes, I suppose I am. For the first time as an adult I'm free to make choices, travel, go where I need to go. There's no one to be there for. Do you know that's why Aunt Connie said she never married? She said she wanted the freedom to follow her own dreams. She said she didn't want to be restricted by someone else's needs and desires. She said it wouldn't have been fair to her or to a husband."

Steven looked at her intensely. "Do you think she ever regretted her decision?"

"I don't know. Constance Greene wasn't the kind to look back and question herself. Still, there were one or two men who asked her, and she did say once that she'd come close to breaking her own resolution. But no, I don't think she regretted a thing."

Steven nodded slowly, his hand slipping off Lila's

arm. He looked down at the sand as her eyes sought the sky.

After a while she noticed him tracing designs in the sand with his finger. Sand clung to his arm, and as he dried, it fell back to the beach. He had strong arms, and Lila was suddenly filled with the desire to feel them around her. She stood quickly, scattering sand, searching for and finding her shoes.

He looked around at her. "What's the rush?"

"I'd better go shower before I start back to work," she said awkwardly and saw the puzzled expression that stole over his face. "Don't worry about me," she added. "I can get back by myself."

He stood effortlessly. "That's okay. I've got a lot of work to do on the book." He pulled on his shirt and his shoes and climbed the rock. Then, taking Lila's hand, he hauled her up to stand beside him. For a second his hand stayed wrapped around hers, his arm encircling her waist to keep her from stepping backward and falling.

As he looked down at her and she raised her face to him, Lila heard the ocean crashing on the beach, felt the breeze tickle her sun-pink cheeks. She thought Steven was going to kiss her, and it seemed like the most natural thing in the world. Their faces moved closer till she could smell the salt on his skin, her heartbeat quickening as she imagined what his warm lips would feel like against hers.

"There you guys are," Jay called.

Startled, they both looked up at once. Jay was on the path far above them, his dark hair slightly ruffled by the wind, his incredible eyes piercing even from that distance. Steven slid his hand from around Lila's waist but kept hold of her hand.

"Let's go see what Jay wants," he said as he started up the path.

Lila trudged along behind him. By the time they got to the top, she was huffing and puffing. Steven, annoyingly, wasn't even breathing hard.

"I thought everyone had deserted me," Jay said.

"Since when do you need company?" Steven asked as he brushed sand off his bare legs.

Jay looked at Lila and smiled. She wished he wouldn't look at her like that, as though they shared some kind of private understanding. The look didn't appear to be lost on Steven, either. He started off toward the trees or, Lila supposed, toward the small building inside the trees.

Lila called out after him. "Thanks for the swim!"

He turned briefly. Jay contrived to have his hand near Lila's cheek, and Steven said, "Anytime," before turning back around.

Lila stepped away from Jay.

He held up a tiny piece of seaweed as though to justify his touch. "Looked pretty cozy down there," he said.

Lila made herself laugh. "I've got to go take a shower."

"I'm sorry I missed it," he said, motioning toward the beach and ignoring her remark about the necessity for a shower.

"You'll have to come next time. The water is cold but invigorating."

Jay put his hands on his waist. "I wasn't referring to the water," he said. "I was thinking more along the lines of your cavorting on the beach."

Lila shook her head. "You're hopeless," she said and, turning, walked toward the house, aware that Jay's gaze was following her every step.

Endora had changed clothes again. "What about this?" she asked. She was wearing a bright purple blouse with three rows of wide ruffles that plunged daringly low. Lila thought the color was hard and brittle and made Endora's skin look sallow. To top it off, huge earrings, shaped like stalks of lilacs, dangled from each ear.

"I've had this blouse for thirty years," Endora said proudly. "Remember, dear, you said to wear something my friends and the boys would recognize."

Lila found her eyes straying to Steven, who was looking down at a stack of papers, his face hidden, but his shoulders trembling ever so slightly. She knew he was laughing.

"I know I did," Lila said. She tilted her head to one side and added, "But you know what? I think the color might be a bit bright. I do so love you in more subdued shades."

Endora sat abruptly on her chair. "I just don't know what to choose," she said.

"Grandmother," Steven said, looking up, "why don't you take Lila upstairs and let her look at your clothes? I bet she'll be able to help you choose something.''

Endora clapped her hands together. "Would you, dear?"

"Happily," Lila agreed.

Endora took Lila's hand and led her up the stairs. They passed the door of the blue room and one that was all gray with accents of lavender—Jay's room, Endora confided—ending up at the end of the hall. Lila wondered which closed door led to Steven's room or if he slept in the small building nestled in the trees.

Endora swung open the door, and it came as no surprise to Lila to find herself in a bedroom that looked lilac, smelled lilac, almost tasted lilac.

The plush carpet ate her shoes. The canopy bed was covered with a printed spread that looked as though someone had painted a flowering lilac bush on fabric. Huge vases of the flowers sat on top of every flat surface except the bed and the floor. What appeared to be an original Matisse hung against the deep-green wallpaper.

As Endora crossed the room and threw open her closet door, Lila stood closer to the painting, admiring it greatly. She turned to see Endora standing in front of a huge closet stuffed with clothes a million shades of purple.

For over an hour they pulled out this, discarded that, ending up at last with a plum-colored gown with a luxuriant sheen Lila was dying to paint, and a gauzy lilac-colored stole they agreed looked heavenly next to the dress. Endora tried them on together, and Lila's face must have reflected how delightful the older woman looked, for Endora quickly turned herself to face the mirror.

"I bought it for my birthday party," Endora said, fidgeting with the simple scalloped neckline. "I don't know, Lila. Don't you think it needs something up here?"

Lila looked at the dressing table. Trailing from one side of the mirror were a dozen or more silk scarves and, from the other, a long piece of purple velvet that was pinned with several silk flowers. She took off an orchid and pinned it on Endora's shoulder, positioning the shawl around her arms.

"That's just right!" Endora cried.

"You look wonderful," Lila told her.

Endora, regarding her reflection, said, "Yes, I do, don't I?"

"We'll start tomorrow, okay?"

"How much time will you need?" Endora asked.

"About an hour for the first sitting, maybe another hour in the afternoon. We'll go slow because I know you're working hard on your book and we're in no rush."

"Yes, my book," Endora said, her smile fading for a second. Lila wondered if Endora was stuck; somewhere at some time she'd read about writer's block. Endora tightened the stole around her arms and faced herself in the mirror. "It's going to be a glorious portrait, isn't it, dear?"

Lila looked over Endora's shoulder. "Yes, it really is."

"And we'll unveil it at my birthday party right before my surprise."

"Your surprise?" Lila asked, adjusting the stole.

Endora's eyes widened; then she giggled. "Our secret, dear," she said.

Steven excused himself immediately after dinner. Lila watched him cross the grass toward the eucalyptus forest, a manila folder in his hands. Endora saw the direction of Lila's gaze and said, "He goes out to work every night after we slave away all afternoon." She paused for a second and, biting her upper lip, added, "I wouldn't have been able to write the last two books without him."

"You could talk into a tape recorder, send the tapes into town to be typed, and get the same results," Jay said.

"That's not true!" Endora snapped.

Jay shrugged elegantly. "You've written hundreds of romances, Grandmother. Steven just records what you say to him."

Endora shook her head. "That's not true, Jay."

"What does he do that a tape recorder couldn't except type? And I already told you a service could perform that tedious chore."

"He's helping me with my thoughts. He keeps me on track. Why, it's almost as though he knows the plot before I do," she added, speaking slowly. It made Lila wonder if this was the first time Endora had actually thought about what it was Steven did for her.

"He reminds me of where I am and what this character said to that character. Before he came, I was ready to quit writing. I thought I'd had enough. But Steven helped me put the book I was working on back together, and then when I started another, he was kind enough to help me again.'' The bewildered look left her face, and she said, ''You may not have noticed it, Jay, but I'm getting old, and sometimes I forget things.''

Jay laughed. ''Not you, Grandmother. You're quicker by far than I am, aren't you?''

''So what?'' she said. ''Who isn't?''

''You cut me to the quick.''

''When are you going to get a job?'' she asked.

Lila felt as though she should discreetly disappear into the woodwork, but upon Endora's question, it grew so quiet she hated to draw attention to herself by moving, so she studied her hands and waited for a good moment to excuse herself.

Jay laughed. ''Are you tired of me sponging off of you?'' he asked. ''No, don't bother answering. As a matter of fact, I have a job interview tomorrow.''

''That's wonderful!'' Endora cried. ''Where? What kind of job?''

''Let's not jinx it by talking about it, okay?''

''But, Jay, you must have some money for tomorrow. I'll get Steven to write you a check—''

''No,'' Jay interrupted. ''I don't like taking money from Steven, even if it's your money, Grandmother.''

''I must have some cash somewhere. Where's my purse? Rose, where's my purse?''

Rose appeared so quickly that Lila wondered if she

had been lurking on the other side of the door, waiting for her summons.

"Yes?" Rose asked.

"Be a saint and find my purse, will you?" Endora asked.

Rose reached to the sideboard behind the table and produced Endora's huge leather bag. "You told me to keep it near you, remember? You said you thought the twice-a-week cleaning woman was stealing from you."

"Oh, that's right." As she dug into her purse for her wallet, Endora looked at Lila and said, "Sometimes I notice I'm a little low right after that girl cleans."

"That's terrible," Lila said.

"I know this sounds like a cliché, but good help is so difficult to find. . . . Ah, here it is, Jay. Now I insist, dear. Take this."

Lila looked away from the exchange of money, but she couldn't help seeing what a thick wad of bills Endora handed her grandson. She ended up looking at Rose, who was looking very sourly at the proceedings.

"And now I must go up to bed," Endora said. "My favorite show is on tonight, and I'm bushed. Rose, bring the TV up to my room so I can watch my show in bed."

As the two old women left the room, Lila heard Rose say, "You've had a television in your room for fifteen years!"

Lila smiled to herself, somewhat startled by the fondness she was beginning to feel for her hostess.

Jay leaned toward Lila. "How about another walk in the moonlight?" he asked.

"No, thanks, Jay—"

"Then how about a drive into town? I know a few dance clubs. There's this one spot—"

"No, not tonight," she said.

He folded his hands and regarded Lila over his fingertips. "You think I'm a shameless no-good who takes money from his little old grandmother, don't you?"

"It's not that. I'm just tired. All I want is a quiet evening in my room."

He smiled. "You don't fool me, Lila Greene, but don't worry your pretty head about Endora. Grandpa left her very well off. Besides, her little books are still being reprinted, and what with the new ones she cranks out—" He stood and added, "If anyone asks, which I'm sure they won't, tell them I've gone into town alone then, will you?"

"Of course."

She watched him leave, then slowly stood. Before she followed, she looked out the window for one last glimpse at the bright lights showing through the branches of the eucalyptus trees.

Chapter Six

THE heroine blushed thirteen times—Lila counted, so she knew—in Endora's first book. It had been re-released in the seventies, so the cover made the book look much newer than it was. But thirteen times!

And the swooning—at the end of every other chapter! But it was a sweet story with a romantic hero, and Lila found herself becoming involved. Despite her original intention of skimming through it quickly so she could dutifully report to Endora, she found herself reading it page by page. It wasn't a long book, and after two hours Lila closed the back cover.

"That was nice," she said aloud.

She picked up a book she'd grabbed from the other end of the row and looked at its cover. No young, daintily draped heroine on this cover! The drawing was bold and concise, a stark picture of a woman in snug jeans, an anchor line trailing from one hand and a gun from the other, the tall mast of a sailboat rising in the distance. The woman's expression said, ''Don't mess with me.'' The title, *Murder in Neon*, was set in block letters.

Lila opened the book, looking for Steven's name in acknowledgment of his help, but the dedication said, *To my handsome Jay,* and she could find no mention of Steven anywhere. It had been published very recently, since the first of the year. Remembering what Steven had said about Endora preferring her earlier books, Lila flipped the book open in the middle and read a few paragraphs, fully intending to put the book aside:

> *Her breath coming in ragged gasps, Jessie hauled in the rubber raft, anxious to stow it aboard the* Ariel *and get the boat under way before the sun came up. It was sluggish, which suggested it had sprung a leak and was now half full of water; she took a flashlight out of her pocket to check out her suspicions.*
>
> *It took her brain a moment to register what she saw in the wobbly stream of light. At first it looked as though a man had climbed into the raft and had fallen asleep. In the instant that momentum carried the raft a foot closer to the boat, Jessie noticed the slash of red across the man's throat, the abandoned, unnatural posture of his body, the pink hue of the water sloshing about his legs.*
>
> *She screamed as the flashlight slipped from her fin-*

gers, plunging beneath the surface of the rolling ocean where it spiraled downward in its waterproof casing.

Lila quickly turned back to the first page and began reading avidly, turning each page almost before she came to the last word on the previous one. She smiled when she read the line about the neon lights reflecting lilac off the gun barrel, then shuddered as one of the murderers fell dead at Jessie's feet. Endora's style had certainly evolved over the years; for one thing, this heroine didn't blush—or swoon—once!

Murder in Neon was a longer book as well, and by the time Lila finished reading it, it was the middle of the night and—as Aunt Connie would have said—she was wound up tighter than a clock. She got out of bed to stretch her legs and crack open the window. She stood there a while, looking out to sea, the breeze caressing her face. The moon was still full and very high because of the hour. It shone directly down, giving the ocean's surface a silver matte appearance. It also partially illuminated the back patio, and Lila's gaze swept over the ghostlike shapes of the tubs of flowers, the familiar table and chairs, the now obviously folded umbrella.

When she saw a movement at the table, a scream leaped up her throat but died in her mouth. A man's shape took form as he got to his feet. Lila stepped to the side, almost sure the man had stopped to look up at her window, which was no doubt the only one to glow in the late hour. She peeked back down a second later, but the man was gone.

To her knowledge, there were only three men on the estate: Jay, Steven, and the cook, whom she had learned during dinner was really named Cook—Andrew Cook, to be precise. Anyway, she thought as she crawled back into bed and turned off her lamp, it wasn't Cook, as he weighed twice as much as Steven or Jay. That meant it was one of them.

Without being able to see their faces or tell their coloring, it was amazing how similar they appeared, especially from above where it was difficult to discern exact measurements. Jay was a little taller perhaps, and Steven a little more muscular, but the differences were slight.

What was either one of them doing sitting out on the patio, in the dark, at three o'clock in the morning? Was Jay worried about his interview, or Steven the direction of his grandmother's book or perhaps his abandoned dreams, whatever they were?

She closed her eyes and was suddenly back on the beach, the sunlight catching in Steven's hair, radiating from his skin. She drifted off to sleep with a kaleidoscope of images arranging themselves in her mind, including the intensity of Jay's gaze as he looked down from his perch atop the cliff.

Endora held her pose far better than Lila had a right to expect—chin high, a delightfully knowing smile on her lips, her eyes snapping. Lila sketched the layout of the drawing quickly on a piece of paper the same size as the forty-eight by thirty-eight-inch canvas she'd stretched earlier that morning. She used swift charcoal lines, defining the angles and planes of her model's head and upper torso down to her lap, where her hands lay one upon the other.

"Lila dear?" Endora said.

Lila softened a line with her thumb. "Hm?"

"Dear, this old body is getting a little stiff."

Lila looked up. "Oh, I'm sorry."

"Has it been an hour yet?"

Lila attended to Endora's beauty mark—wasn't it higher today than yesterday?—before answering. "Yes, fine. Fine." She walked away from the drawing, stretching her own back and shoulders. "Maybe this afternoon?"

Endora stood slowly, regal-looking in her beautiful gown. "Yes, this afternoon I can spare another hour. But I must get along with my book. Dear, one hates to pry, but when are you actually going to paint something?"

Lila laughed softly. "This afternoon perhaps. This is the last preliminary drawing, I promise."

"May I see?"

Lila held the paper a little distance from Endora so she could get an idea of the composition. The older woman shrugged. "I hope the painting looks better than that!" she said.

"It will, I promise."

The door opened, and both women turned to see Steven. "How's it going?" he asked.

Lila said it was going fine. She looked back at the paper and added a line here, smudged a line there.

"Grandmother, the florist is here. She wants to discuss the flowers for your party."

Endora squealed with delight. She hefted her skirt and hurried past Lila, who was busy propping the paper back onto the easel. Lila heard Steven say something about them waiting for Endora in the study, but in truth she was concentrating on her sketch. She backed away from it, attempting to gain perspective. She'd all but forgotten about Steven until she backed into him.

"I like it," he said above her head, his hands wrapped around her arms. Her back was to him. She twirled around to face him.

"Sorry. I guess I forgot you were still in the room."

"How flattering," he said with a grin.

She turned to face the canvas again. The proportions were fine, she thought. She would paint Endora life-size, as it both presented the most realistic appearance and was the most natural path between the subject and her artist's hand and eye. She turned and was startled anew to find Steven watching her.

"Don't tell me," he said dryly. "You'd forgotten I was here *again*?"

Lila smiled. "I notice you do the same thing when you're writing in Endora's study," she said.

He frowned. "I don't write. I take dictation."

"Not according to Endora," Lila said.

"Wait a second. What did Endora say to you?"

"To me and Jay. Before he told us about the job interview he has today, we were talking about writing." Lila's voice faltered as she recalled the derisive way in which Jay had spoken of Steven's help.

"And?" Steven coaxed.

"What? Oh, nothing really. Your grandmother just told us that you do a lot more than copy her words. She says you keep her on track. Let's see . . . yes, that's right . . . she said that you seem to know the plot almost before she does!"

Steven stared at Lila until she was prompted to ask, "Is something wrong?"

He shook his head.

She held up her charcoal-stained hands. "If you'll get the doorknob for me, I'll go wash up for lunch."

He opened the door, but as she passed him, he caught her arm. "Lila, what did Jay say to all this?"

"To what your grandmother said? As I recall, nothing. In fact, right after she sang your praises, she asked him if he was ever going to get a job."

"How delightful for you," Steven said, breaking into a smile.

"Right. That's when he informed her about the job interview." She didn't tell him about the exchange of money, but she did say, "Steven, what do you think about Fay or Rae, or whatever the twice-a-week maid's name is, stealing from Endora's purse?"

"You mean Kaye Wallis? Who said she steals?"

"Endora."

"I had no idea—"

"Then I shouldn't have said anything."

"I'll talk to Endora about it."

"She says good help is hard to find."

Steven laughed, and the sound was like water tripping over rocks. "Well, I'm sure she's right, but surely we can find someone who doesn't rob her. Kaye, huh? Who would have believed it?''

Lila thought of the mumbling woman and thought it wasn't too hard a stretch to imagine her sneaking money out of an untended purse. Steven dropped his hand, which had stayed on Lila's arm while they talked, and she went upstairs to wash.

Lunch was on the patio again, and this time everyone was there. Endora declared it was a victory party to celebrate Jay's new job, which he still refused to explain. She'd changed into a lavender jumpsuit and talked excitedly about her birthday-party plans while the rest of them helped themselves to some kind of enchilada dish.

''The flowers are going to be enchanting,'' Endora declared. ''Gladiolus the exact color of my engraved invitations—''

''Speaking of invitations,'' Jay interrupted, ''I never have seen one.''

''No one around here has except Endora and Rose,'' Steven said. ''Grandmother was quite secretive about it.''

''I'd love to see one,'' Lila said.

''It's not as though there won't be a few at the party, Grandmother,'' Steven pointed out. ''Whatever you're trying to hide will be out of the bag soon.''

''Very well,'' Endora said. ''I just so happen to have one because of the florist.'' She dug around in her pocket and then, with a flourish befitting a magician who successfully produces a rabbit out of a hat, came up with one of her invitations.

The paper was thick and expensive and—*surprise,* Lila thought—lilac-colored. On the outside was an exquisite silk screening of a mass of flowers. Lila opened it and read the inside: *You are cordially invited to a party celebrating the eighty-sixth birthday of the famous author Endora Yolette. In honor of the occasion, a portrait by noted artist Constance Greene will be unveiled, followed by a surprise announcement from Endora Yolette herself.*

Endora pointed a purple fingernail at Lila's aunt's name. "I didn't know she was dead when I had these printed," she explained.

"But what if she had refused to come?" Lila asked, startled into abruptness. "Quite frankly, Endora, there aren't too many artists who could drop everything and travel seven hundred miles on the spur of the moment."

"Not even for me?" Endora said patiently. "I knew she'd come and paint my portrait, dear."

Lila looked at Steven, who took the invitation from her hands and began reading it for himself.

"But she hasn't come, Grandmother," Jay said, looking over Steven's shoulder. "You were just lucky Lila arrived."

"And the invitations should be reprinted," Steven pointed out, "with Lila's name on them."

"Whatever for?" Endora asked.

"So she'll get the credit," Jay said.

"But it's too late, Steven, you know that. You sent them out yourself!"

"But you wouldn't let me look at them. You were very sneaky about it, Endora. You and Rose sealed them in their envelopes before you gave them to me to address. If I'd had any idea of this scheme—''

''I wanted to surprise you,'' Endora interrupted. ''But I see what you mean about poor Lila. It's like my book *Romance on the Stage* when the understudy has to go on for the famous actress and does a much better job, but because she's wearing such a heavy wig, no one knows she's really who she is—''

''What if we have the printers make up an announcement about Lila being the artist? We could get someone to hand them out to people as they arrived.'' This suggestion came from Steven, and Endora clapped her hands together. ''Perfect, dear! You're so brilliant. Isn't he, Jay?''

''A veritable genius,'' Jay said.

''It's better than nothing, anyway,'' Steven told Lila.

''Of course it is,'' Endora insisted. Lila noted that no one had responded to the ''surprise'' part of the invitation.

''The cleaner delivered your dinner jacket,'' Jay said in what Lila took to be a valiant attempt to change the subject.

Steven said, ''Good,'' without looking at his cousin.

''And Donna Ransom called. She said she'll be ready by eight o'clock tonight.''

Steven looked swiftly at Lila. ''Thanks, Jay.''

''Such a spectacular girl, Steven,'' Endora said as she sipped iced tea.

''She's a real looker, and her father is loaded,'' Jay

added. "Just about the ideal girl, wouldn't you say, cousin?"

"Please!" Steven snapped. "Give it a rest, will you?"

Jay laughed. He looked at Lila and said, "I haven't formally thanked you for accepting my rather tardy and once-removed invitation, so I do it now, pretty Lila. Thank you."

"Thank you for what?"

"For going with me tonight."

She stared at Jay with wide eyes. "I have no idea what you're talking about."

"Grandmother?" Jay said. "You told me you asked her this morning."

Endora coughed into her napkin. "Well, I meant to. Anyway, of course she'll go."

"Go where?" Lila asked.

"The Shelter Island Yacht Club dance, of course."

"But I couldn't—"

"You're hardly giving her much notice," Steven said as he folded his napkin.

"This is all my fault," Endora cried. "I meant to ask her first thing like I told you I would, but we got busy with the portrait, and then before lunch, when you asked me if I'd talked to Lila, I said yes because of course I had, don't you see?"

"It's just a stupid dance," Steven said.

"Easy for you to say with Donna all hot to dance the night away in your arms." Jay looked at Lila and explained. "This dance has been in the works for weeks, of course, and Melissa Dupont had agreed to go with me. She canceled last night because of illness, so before I left this morning, I asked Grandmother to ask you if you'd consider going with me.''

Lila said, ''Oh—''

''There won't be too many single women at this affair. Please, consider it, Lila.''

For some reason Lila found herself glancing at Steven. He was staring at his empty plate.

''Oh, dear, do go,'' Endora said. ''Steven has had plans to go with Donna forever, but poor Jay's plans fell through at the last moment, and if I weren't so absentminded, I would have had time to talk you into going before now. For my sake, dear, do go.''

''Poor Jay'' leaned close to Lila. ''I revow my gentlemanly oath of conduct,'' he said. ''Come on, a night out will be good for you.''

''Maybe she'd rather not pinch-hit for another woman,'' Steven suggested.

Lila glared at him, thinking, *Thanks a lot, Steven, for putting it so nicely.* She looked back at Jay and said, ''I'd love to go, but it's only fair to warn you I don't have anything to wear, at least nothing fancy enough to complement a tuxedo.''

Endora giggled. ''Silly girl. Fancy clothes are my department. Don't you worry, Jay, she'll be presentable.''

''Lila would be presentable in a gunnysack,'' he said.

From her left side, Lila heard Steven mutter under his breath. It sounded like, ''Oh, brother!''

*   *   *

The afternoon saw the first strokes of paint touch the canvas. Endora was fidgety, however, so Lila did little more than draw the general shape of the pose. She would have preferred to keep on working, the words of one of her professors ringing in her ears like bells tolling. "Do the painting in one sitting!" he'd insisted, but Lila had found that there were as many ways to approach a portrait as there were artists and subjects.

"We'll tackle this in earnest tomorrow," Lila said after Endora moved for the twentieth time.

Endora stood at once. "Good. Let's go upstairs and choose your dress."

Lila was staring at the canvas. "Pardon me?"

"You really are driven, aren't you? I see you here and there, sketching all the time. Well, never mind. Come along—we need to pick out a dress for tonight, and then Steven and I simply must work on that book for a while. Why my agent or the editor aren't breathing fire down our necks is simply beyond me. Lila dear, come along."

Lila tore herself away from her work, though turning her back on a beginning project was more difficult than she'd have imagined. "I set up the turpentine in the garage," she said. "I'll have to wash out the brush before I play dress-up."

"Just hurry," Endora said impatiently.

A little while later Lila stood in front of the big mirrors in Endora's room and looked at herself in a pale lilac-colored sequined gown. The neckline plunged, the back plunged, and, what was worse, there wasn't enough of Lila to compensate for all the plunging.

"I never realized how much smaller you are than I am. You really are short, aren't you?" Endora said.

Lila could think of nothing to say, so she shrugged. "Do you have anything a little more understated, perhaps something with a higher neckline?"

Endora tore through her closet like a dirt devil in a plowed field. She emerged a moment later with a sleeveless white tuniclike dress made of silk cut from a cloud. It was modestly split up one side and, best of all, the neckline wasn't out to make a statement. It was way too long, but Endora tore a gold cord from another dress and gave it to Lila, who used it to tie around her waist. A little tug here and there brought the hem up to where she could walk.

"I've had this dress for ages, and you know what? I don't believe I've ever worn it."

"Then I couldn't—"

"Fiddle-faddle, of course you can. It's not purple, but nothing is perfect, and besides, white becomes you. Besides, I daresay I'd look like a well-dressed ghost in this dress. Now, what's missing? Oh, of course! Shoes, you need shoes," she announced and once again disappeared into the closet. She emerged with a pair of gold heels, but they were far too big.

"I have a pair of gold slippers my aunt gave me," Lila said suddenly. She dashed to her room and came back with the slippers.

Lila thought the slippers looked fine, but Endora was obviously displeased. At last, she scrunched up her purple lips and said, "I guess they'll do. The hem is long enough to hide them."

"I think so," Lila agreed. She pulled off the dress and put it back on the hanger. "Endora, who is this Donna Ransom?"

"The general's daughter. I will tell you something in the strictest of confidences, Lila. I can trust you?"

"Of course."

"The general pinched my fanny once!"

Lila smiled.

"Honestly, dear child, he truly did. And I let him have it too!" She sat on the edge of the bed and added, "Of course, don't let this influence what you think about his daughter. She reminds me of one of my heroines—you know, all legs and full lips and a wild mane of hair. Delightful girl. And she and Steven look perfect together. I think that's important, don't you?" Propping her hands on her knees and leaning forward, she added, "Don't tell Steven, but I've got a bet with myself that he and Donna will get married one of these days!"

Lila was surprised to find how shocked she was by this confidence. She said, "I have to do something with my hair. You'll excuse me, won't you?"

"Certainly, dear. You and Jay will look charming together, just charming."

And they did, Lila had to admit a few hours later as she caught sight of their reflection in the glass of the Yacht Club doors. They were both dark-haired and slender, he tall and graceful, she petite. He was wearing a white dinner jacket, so even their clothes complemented each other.

The Shelter Island Yacht Club was a beautiful place for a nighttime dance, Lila thought as she walked into the main room with Jay. Large, rich with varnished wood and lit subtly with flickering lamps, it managed to be romantic and nautical at the same time. A band played at one end while clusters of beautifully dressed people chatted together around the perimeter of the wooden dance floor. A dozen or so couples were dancing, their bodies swaying in time to the mellow music.

"This is very nice," Lila said to the commodore of the Yacht Club, no other than General Ransom himself. He was a distinguished-looking man of sixty-five or so, one of those full-bodied, white-haired, flush-faced kinds who instantly reminded Lila of the bank presidents she'd painted to fulfill her aunt's contract.

"Endora has mentioned your name," Lila told him.

"Lovely woman," he said. He was so stuffy, it was impossible for Lila to imagine he'd actually relaxed to the point of pinching. "Tell me, my dear, have you met my daughter yet?"

"Not yet."

"I believe her young man took her out for a light supper before bringing her here." He cast Jay a rather pointed look, which Lila wasn't sure how to read.

Jay just smiled and, guiding Lila by the arm, moved her toward the dance floor. Lila was hardly aware of the music; all she could hear were the words *her young man*.

"Shall we?" Jay asked.

"What? Oh, yes, of course. It's why we're here, right?"

"Right," he said. "Well, what did you think of Endora's 'old billy goat'?"

"He seems a little uptight for what she says he did."

"You mean the celebrated pinch? I gather he'd had a little too much wine that night."

Lila nodded. As preoccupied as she was, she found that after a while the music and soft lights got to her. Jay was a very good dancer, sure of foot and smooth, his arms strong.

"I'm having a hard time tonight," Jay said as he ran his hands down Lila's bare arms.

She looked up, tilting her head back to see his face. "In what way?" she asked.

"In keeping my promise, Lila Greene. The fact of the matter is that I'd like to kiss you, and I have the feeling you'd like me to go ahead and do it."

Lila laughed softly. "You're always telling me how you think I feel about things. Trust me to have the sense to tell you myself, okay?"

"Must I? Okay, I must. Have you noticed the saxophone player ogling you?"

Lila turned to face the band. The saxophone player was young and handsome, but he seemed totally involved with his music. "He is not."

"Sure he is. Not when you're looking, of course. Don't you think this dance is kind of boring?"

"I think it's very nice."

"Nice—translation, boring. Let's go."

"Not yet," Lila said. "I'm enjoying myself. Why don't you tell me all about your interview today?"

"More boring stuff."

"Or why you're keeping your new job such a secret. Let's see. Are you the new pizza delivery boy, or maybe a hit man with the mob?"

"Both," he said, smiling, and Lila gave it up. She didn't realize how often she looked at the big, open arch of the dance room until she saw Steven framed in the doorway.

He was dressed in a black dinner jacket and white shirt, a red carnation fastened to his lapel. With his sandy-colored hair and tan skin, he gave a strong impression of outdoor formality as his gaze traveled the dark room. Lila's heart stopped beating as his eyes finally found hers and for an eon stayed locked in place, diving into her soul, taking her breath away.

Then Jay twirled her around until her back was to the doorway. By the time she was turned yet again, Steven had been joined by a long-legged blonde.

"They're here," Jay whispered in her ear.

"Are they?" Lila asked. She looked where Jay pointed as though it were her first glimpse, and then she joined him in waving. *Ah, the games we play*, she thought.

Lila saw Donna tug Steven toward the dance floor; then she became aware Jay was speaking to her.

"The general really likes Steve," he said.

Lila said, "What?"

"Donna's father. He thinks the world of Steve. Thinks he's upright and respectable."

"Oh."

Jay laughed. "Don't worry about it, little Lila. Donna is as conceited as I am. She thinks Steve is handsome and virile, but I can't imagine Steve sees anything in her beyond her obvious physical attributes."

This was supposed to reassure her? "I don't know what you're talking about," she insisted.

"Okay. If that's the way you want it."

"That's the way it is. I've only been here three days. Give me a chance."

"You promise to give me one?" Jay quipped, and then he released his grip on Lila. "Donna! You look absolutely stunning tonight!"

Lila turned to see that Jay had guided them across the floor before the music stopped. She looked at Donna and saw just what she expected—decent bones, good color, nice tilt to the blue-gray eyes. Then her gaze traveled up to Steven's face, and she saw the familiar strong jaw and straight brows over deep-set green eyes. He said, "Hello, Lila."

She smiled, suddenly shy.

"Isn't there any champagne around here?" Donna asked. "I mean, don't you think it should be flowing? I *am* the commodore's daughter, you know, and I think the least Daddy could have done was make sure there were adequate supplies—"

"Shall we go check into it?" Jay interrupted. He looked at Lila as the music began again. "You wouldn't mind?"

"Of course not," she said.

''Steve will watch out for you. Come on, Donna. Let's find champagne!''

For a few seconds Lila and Steven stood side by side in the middle of the dance floor, neither one of them looking at the other. Someone bumped into Lila, said, ''Sorry,'' and danced away. Steven opened his arms, and with a sense of the inevitable, Lila stepped into his embrace.

He wasn't as smooth a dancer as his cousin, but Lila barely noticed. Why was it, she mused, that one handsome man's touch could elicit nothing and another's could set nerve endings on fire? She felt his warm breath on her forehead, smelled the after-shave on his throat, sensed his heartbeat under her cheek.

They didn't look at each other or exchange a single word; they just moved around the dance floor in perfect harmony, Lila's dark head tucked neatly under Steven's chin, his arm wrapped tightly around her back. Lila had no sense of time. She didn't know if one song played or two or even three. All she was aware of was Steven and that she wanted it to last forever.

And then the music really did stop. She stepped away from him, her cheeks flushed, and found his expression as baffled as hers surely was.

Jay appeared with Donna on one side and a waiter on the other. The waiter was holding a tray of champagne glasses, and each person took one. After they had sipped the wine, Donna asked Steven to dance with her, and Jay took Lila back to the table by the smoky windows.

Lila turned away from watching Steven and looked

out toward San Diego Bay. She couldn't actually see the bay as it was covered with boats, and from her vantage point inside the club, all she could see were masts. Hundreds, maybe thousands of them.

"You've really got it bad," Jay said idly.

Lila looked at him and smiled. "There you go again."

"And he's got it just as bad as you do."

"May we please change the subject?"

Just then Donna and Steven approached their table. The four of them sat together, but while Jay and Donna gossiped about mutual friends and drank copious amounts of champagne, Steven and Lila said hardly a word. When Donna convinced Steven to dance with her again, Lila turned to Jay and found him laughing softly. She smiled and looked at her hands.

Three young men Lila had never seen before showed up and found more chairs. They told jokes, made plans for later in the evening, and made friendly passes at Lila until Jay asked her to dance again. Once more Lila found herself twirling around the dance floor in Jay's capable arms. She didn't see Steven and Donna anywhere.

"What do you want, Lila Greene?" Jay asked out of the blue.

"What do you mean?"

"Tonight, this very moment. What's your heart's desire?"

She shook her head.

"Come on, don't be shy."

"The truth? I don't know. I guess I'd like to be sure about . . . things."

"Like your feelings?" he asked.

"Yes. And about my work and the direction I should go. Jay, have you ever wanted something so badly it frightens you?"

"No," he answered at once. "Not me. I'm the cool one, the one who takes each day as it comes."

"You're not as indifferent as all that."

He laughed. "Don't let your opinions get around. They might jeopardize my reputation as the free-wheeling Yolette man. How about tonight, right this minute? If you could have anything, what would it be?"

Lila smiled. The one "thing" she wanted was at the dance with another woman. She said, "Nothing."

"Tilt, wrong answer. Come on, name it."

"You asked for it. I'd like to go home, I guess. Now I'm being rude."

"Not rude," he assured her. "I dragged you here as a pinch hitter, remember?"

Lila touched her forehead to Jay's shoulder.

She felt him move and then heard a soft jangle. When she looked up, she saw he'd produced his car keys. "Shall I take you home?"

"You don't want to leave yet," Lila said as she recognized Donna dancing with one of Jay's friends. "Besides, you've had too much to drink to start driving."

"You heard me make plans with Jeff and Rob to go out to a few clubs after this dinosaur of a dance is finished. Come with us; you'll have fun. And don't frown at me like that, because Jeff hasn't been drinking at all, and he's the driver.'' He kissed her on the cheek and added, ''From the looks of things, Donna will be going too.''

Lila looked where he gestured. Donna was dancing with the man Jay had introduced as Rob. She had her head tilted back, her ''wild mane of hair,'' as Endora would have called it, trailing down her back while Rob planted a kiss on her throat. Lila looked around the room for Steven.

''He left,'' Jay said.

She looked up at Jay. ''I'm not much of a date, am I?''

''I'll get you a ride home,'' he said with a surprisingly tender smile.

''Jay, since Rob is going to drive, will you let me borrow your car? I can get myself home.''

''Grandmother would nail my hide to a wall if she saw that I let you come home alone.''

Lila glanced at her watch. ''It's almost midnight. Endora will be asleep.''

''You wouldn't mind?'' he asked.

''Not at all. In fact, I wouldn't feel so guilty about wrecking your evening.''

He folded her hand over his keys. ''You're a great date, though maybe not the perfect date for me.''

''A ray of honesty?''

''A small ray.''

They stopped dancing. It took a while, but eventually a group of six, including Donna, walked Lila out to

Jay's car, saw her safely ensconced, and left. Lila sat behind the wheel for several minutes, then on impulse got out of the car and walked toward the yacht-club docks.

It was a lovely night, and though the sky was city lit, Lila saw several stars and a high moon. The wind had come up unexpectedly, and she was slightly chilled in the thin dress, but the walk among the beautiful boats more than compensated. She stopped to admire a pretty sloop when she heard sounds from across the dock. Turning, she saw a man bent over a dock line and heard the subdued noise of an inboard engine.

"Are you really going out at night?" Lila asked, announcing her presence. She'd been standing in the shadow of a dock box, and she moved out into the better light.

The man stood up abruptly, the bow line in his hand. "Lila?"

"Steven?"

"Where's Jay?"

"Gone. With Donna and a few others. Everyone thought you'd gone home."

"Why didn't you go with them?"

Lila took a long time answering. "You know why," she said at last.

For several seconds they stared at each other; then Steven said, "Will you come with me?"

She didn't hesitate. She wasn't sure exactly what he meant; she didn't care. "Yes," she said and walked across the dock.

Chapter Seven

"IT has to be fate," Steven declared as he tucked Lila into a corner of the cockpit. "Fate that brought you down the right dock at the right time. You're cold—wait here." He disappeared down below into the cabin and emerged with his dinner jacket, which he insisted she wear. He was dressed in his slacks and formal shirt, the suspenders jauntily crisscrossing his back.

"Fate," Lila repeated under her breath as she wrapped herself in the jacket. The carnation ended up under her nose, and she took an appreciative sniff.

Steven easily guided the boat out of the tight confines of the marina. The motor made the hull vibrate slightly as she sliced through the calm, black water. Lila was enchanted with the fairy-tale appearance of the city as they slowly made their way toward the dark expanse of water that was the bay.

"That's Shelter Island to your left," Steven said, and, after they passed the tip, "Look to your right. That's the Naval Supply Center." Steven turned the boat left; then after giving Lila a brief lesson in turning the wheel the wrong direction to go the right way, he moved along the deck toward the front mast. Soon a huge white triangle filled with air, and Lila felt the boat's hull lean toward the water.

"Steven!" she yelled.

"You're doing fine!" he yelled back. "Don't be scared."

Easier said than done, Lila thought as the boat leaned even more. The engine exhaust was sputtering behind her; the wheel seemed to have a definite mind of its own.

And then Steven was back in the cockpit, hoisting the smaller aft sail. He flipped a switch, and the engine died, and suddenly the boat was moving swiftly at an angle to the wind. Lila felt a surge of wonder course through her veins.

"It's wonderful!" she said. "Oh, Steven, what's her name?"

"*Ariel*," he said.

"And how long is she?"

"Forty-two feet."

"She's a ketch, right?"

"Right. She's a double ender. She was built in 1955

of cedar over oak frames. She's heavy, not very fast, but a great cruiser.''

Lila smiled into Steven's jacket. He showed her how to keep the wheel balanced so that the sails stayed full, assuring her the task would be much easier in the daytime when you could see things better. Thanks to the deck lights, Lila was able to see a bit, but Steven switched these off, leaving only one small light atop the main mast and the two running lights burning— green on the starboard, red on the port. He fidgeted with the various lines and finally sat back in the cockpit, so close to Lila his knees touched hers.

''You really like it, don't you?'' he asked.

''Oh, yes. I don't think I've felt like this since I was a little kid with a great imagination. I used to watch my dad sail kites, and sometimes I imagined I was on the kite, looking down at the earth. I was very interested in color, and I fancied, aloft like that, that I'd be able to see every little shade of every color in the rainbow. Let me tell you, my first view out of an airplane window was a vast disappointment.''

''Don't get too comfortable,'' Steven said. ''We're going to have to tack or end up on North Island, smack dab in the middle of the Naval air station.'' He scrambled to his feet and hauled on this line, released that one, telling Lila what to do in the meantime. When the boat was safely traveling in the other direction, he sat back down.

''Do you want me to take the wheel?'' he asked.

''Not unless I'm doing something wrong.''

''No. You're not doing anything wrong. Ease off a

little. Listen to the sails—when they flap and flutter, it's time to correct your course, just a little, see? Perfect. You're a natural, aren't you?''

''Am I?'' Lila asked, giggling.

He laughed too. ''Where does your father live now?''

''He died, he and Mother both, back when I was ten years old. A drunk driver got them. I guess that's why I'm so concerned about drinking and driving. Anyway, Aunt Connie raised me.''

''No wonder you were so close to her,'' he said and added quietly, ''No wonder you want to be just like her.''

''She was wonderful. She supported me, educated me, gave me every advantage she could afford. I adored her.''

Steven put his hands on Lila's as she gripped the wheel. He moved them a little to the left and, sure enough, Lila could feel *Ariel* settle into a more comfortable course. Pretty soon they had to tack again, and then again until gradually Lila saw an enchanting bridge floating above the bay.

''Coronado,'' Steven said. ''Have you noticed the wind is dying down?''

Lila had noticed. It was harder and harder to keep the sails full of air. While she watched, he lowered the sails, restarted the engine, and motored the boat closer to shore. Lila helped with the setting of the anchor and, once it was done, stared at the city of Coronado, which looked, in the dark, like most any other city except that there were very few lights on shore directly opposite them.

"That's the golf course," Steven said when she asked about it. "Let's just stay here until the wind comes up again."

"Fine with me," Lila agreed.

"Would you like to come below? I'll make coffee."

Lila hiked Endora's dress up around her knees and carefully made her way down the ladder to the inside of the boat. She followed Steven along a very short hall into the main cabin. A kerosene lamp was lit and swung gently from its hook in the ceiling. She looked around the interior and found everything looked very functional, at least to her nautically ignorant eyes.

"Go ahead and look around," Steven said as he dug in a cupboard.

"Okay." There was a cabin in the bow of the boat. On one side was a bed heaped with blankets and pillows, and on the other side, a low seat with drawers underneath. One drawer was slightly ajar, and Lila looked inside. What she saw confused her, so she looked more closely and finally figured out she was looking at a portable computer housed in a dark-gray plastic case.

That mystery solved, she moved aft of the bow cabin and came upon a small bathroom and across from that, a locker for hanging clothes—at least she supposed that was what it was intended for as there was a rod across the top. Steven had stuffed it full of big, brightly colored bags which she assumed held different sails.

The main cabin was next, and the round wooden

main mast came through the top of the cabin and disappeared under the floor, leaving about six and a half
feet of it smack in the middle of the cabin. A small
table was attached to half the mast, and around this
were upholstered seats backed with shelves crammed
with books. The galley was next, with a navigation
station across from it, and lastly, the owner's cabin,
with another bed and more built-in drawers.

Lila returned to the main cabin. "What's the smell
down here?" she asked.

Steven turned his back to the hiss of the stove. "Let's
see. I had a bit of dry rot recently, which I treated with
a lovely little product I call green death, but then again,
you may be smelling diesel fuel, mildew, or just plain
old boat. It's hard to tell."

"A veritable potpourri," she said as she seated herself at the table. As she watched Steven make coffee,
she decided this was where she wanted to paint him,
here aboard his boat. He looked younger, happier,
more content here than anywhere else she'd seen him.
And handsomer, she realized.

He handed her a mug and sat down beside her with
a mug of his own. The boat moved gently on her
anchor; Lila could hear tiny waves slap the hull. She
took a sip of coffee and sighed.

"This is nice," she said.

"I've been down here a thousand times," Steven
said softly, "but it's never seemed as warm or welcoming as it does tonight. That must be because of
you, Lila."

She smiled at him. ''It's because you're so relieved not to be at that dreadful dance.''

''With that dreadful woman,'' Steven added. ''That's not fair—Donna isn't dreadful. She's actually a very nice person; it's just that we're nothing alike.''

''I hear opposites attract,'' Lila mused, taking another sip.

''I hear that, too, but I'm not sure I believe it. The thing is that Donna is no more interested in me than I am in her. Her father is the one who roped me into taking her, and we both did it just to get him off our backs. She got rid of me as soon as she could, thank goodness.''

''You needn't explain to me.''

''I know, I know. But I felt bad about calling you a pinch hitter for Jay's broken date. The truth of the matter was that if I couldn't take you to that stupid dance, I didn't want anyone to take you.''

Lila laughed. ''Jay's not interested in me. Not really.''

''Don't count on it.''

''What do you have against Jay, Steven? I know he's impulsive and a little bit of a scamp, but he seems harmless enough to me.''

''You wouldn't understand.''

''Try me.'' When he still didn't answer, she stood, impatient with his silence. She walked across the cabin to a row of pictures fixed securely to one of the bulkheads; most of them were of *Ariel* under sail. From the exotic backgrounds, it was clear the boat had sailed to faraway places.

"That one was taken in Tahiti in 1959," Steven said. "The former owners took *Ariel* around the world."

"How thrilling!"

"Yes," he said with such a glow in his eyes that Lila could almost feel his desires. She suddenly knew what he'd meant about abandoned dreams: This boat represented his. To test her theory, she asked, "How long have you had *Ariel*?"

"About two years."

"Since before you went to live with Endora?"

"That's right." The glow faded from his eyes, and he stared into his mug.

"You bought her after you quit the advertising business?"

He nodded. "About every penny I had went into buying and equipping her. I bought her in Seattle, and after I got her ready, I sailed her down the coast, intending on going south to Mexico and then down through the Panama Canal. . . . It doesn't matter now."

"But you visited your grandmother, and you decided her needs outweighed your plans, is that it?"

He shrugged. "May we talk about something else?"

"Of course."

He looked up at her, and for a while they stared at each other. Lila was wondering why Steven didn't just hire someone to help Endora—she wasn't that cantankerous, and surely a secretary could be found who could handle the work. She didn't know what he was thinking, wasn't sure she wanted to. One thing was certain, however—whatever magic had been in the air was gone, and, soon after, they pulled in the anchor and silently motored back to the marina.

This time Lila was sure of it. Endora's beauty mark, which had started out on her right cheekbone, was now on the left-hand side. She had proof it wasn't moving around only in her own imagination because she'd drawn it. And now, facing the canvas, her palette set out, paintbrush in hand, there was the beauty mark on the wrong side!

What to do? Would Endora take offense if Lila asked about it? *I'll leave it off entirely,* Lila decided, *and paint it on last thing wherever she decides to wear it that particular day.*

"Have you ever heard of Edward Booker?" Endora asked. She was in her gown, netlike stole posed just so, chin high, hands folded. Lila started painting in the soft guidelines for the facial features.

"Hm?"

"Edward Booker. Do pay attention, dear. He's the editor of that charming little magazine *Art Today.*"

Lila looked at her model. "Keep your chin up, Endora. Yes, of course I've heard of Edward Booker."

"He's a dear friend."

Lila nodded and, concerned only with her painting, said, "How nice."

"Yes. He's coming to the party."

Lila looked up, her expression startled.

"I knew that would get your attention! I told you important people would come to view my portrait!"

Lila swallowed and went back to work. *Art Today*

was a pretentious little art magazine with a limited following, taken seriously mainly by people impressed by important-sounding articles they couldn't understand. What was startling wasn't the prospect of being reviewed by Edward Booker but of seeing the man again.

Lila's memories of him were hazy and indistinct. She'd been twelve the summer they met, and he'd been nothing more than just one of Aunt Connie's friends visiting for the afternoon. It wasn't until years later that Aunt Connie admitted he'd asked her to marry him and she'd refused.

Since then, he'd never once mentioned Constance Greene's name in his magazine. He'd never reviewed one of her shows or done an article on any of her work. In a slim field of ''experts'' who viewed Constance Greene's work ''minimal and unimportant,'' his was the loudest voice because of its silence.

There was no doubt in Lila's mind that Edward Booker would judge her work similarly uninspired. How would Endora take this news? Thankfully, by the time he arrived, the portrait would be complete, and she would be paid and ready to leave.

Leave? To go where? Lila pushed that thought aside and concentrated on indicating the placement of Endora's hands.

An hour later Endora stood abruptly. ''Time's up,'' she announced.

Lila looked up from the canvas. There was a lot she could do with the background and the flowers that didn't require Endora's presence, and she said, "You'll be back this afternoon?"

"Yes, yes, I suppose so. To tell you the truth, I wouldn't have thought having my portrait painted would be such a tedious chore."

Lila smiled and said, "Aunt Connie would have planted you in that chair and not let you leave until she was finished."

Endora's purple lips scrunched together. "Then I'm glad you're the one who's here. Well, if I hurry, maybe Steven and I can get an hour or so in on the book before lunch." She swept by Lila, not even pausing to peruse the painting, which was just as well with Lila.

At the door she turned and said, "By the way, Lila, what did you think of my books?"

As though Lila had had time to read them all! "The first one was very romantic," she said. "And the last one provided such a contrast. It's obvious that you've grown a lot as a writer." Was that the right thing to say?

Apparently not. Endora's hand fluttered around her throat for a moment. "Yes, yes, quite," she said and left quickly.

Lila ate lunch alone that day. Rose explained that Jay was in town because of his new job and that Steven and Endora were closeted in the study, hard at work on the new book. Lila ate and then, after fetching her sketchbook and pencil, settled down on the bluff and drew the beach below. After that she made a quick sketch of Endora's back patio, then moved closer to the eucalyptus trees and drew the little white-and-red house. There was a wonderful trellis of jasmine next to the red door, and Lila ventured close enough to sketch that as well.

The windows were shuttered, and Lila instantly thought of the man who kept them that way. Was Steven as shuttered as his house, as closed? Was that the reason he was so reticent in response to her questions? What did she know about him except that his cousin said he was tight with Endora's money? He seemed generous to Lila, but she couldn't deny that he aroused all sorts of emotions in her that made her a poor judge of his character.

Most of all, she wondered as she drew the little anchor door knocker, why did he stay here instead of leading his own life? Was he afraid, as she'd been after graduation from college? He'd said that she didn't seem like the type to be frightened of her own future. Was he?

Lila closed her eyes and thought of the midnight sail. So many senses were recalled—the smell of the water; the taste of the salt; the sight of the sails in the moonlight; the sound of water rushing by the hull; the feel of the smooth, wooden wheel in her hands— that for a second she was there again, with Steven, on the threshold of something ambiguous but tantalizing. The sound of a nearby footfall on a dry leaf instantly shattered the recollections, and Lila opened her eyes to see Steven standing before her.

She dropped her pencil.

He leaned down and picked it up, craning his neck

a little to see what she'd drawn. What he saw was a collage of his house and the trees, the flowers, and the door knocker.

"Very charming," he said. "Were you coming to visit me?"

"I knew you were lunching in the study with Endora," she told him. "I've often admired this little house, so I decided to take the opportunity my free time afforded me and doodle some."

"Doodle? I'll show you the pad by my telephone sometime, and you'll see doodling. That"—and he gestured toward her paper—"should be framed and hung on a wall."

"Thank you," Lila said, wondering why they were so formal with each other. She added, "I really enjoyed our sail last night."

"Me too. I hope it won't be our last."

"So do I." They went back to staring, something Lila was beginning to think summed up their relationship so far, until Steven sighed.

"Would you like a peek inside?" he asked.

"Very much."

To her surprise, he unlocked the door. She was surprised because she could see no real reason to lock it in the first place. She followed him into a dimly lit room which was blessedly free of purple furniture, carpet, and drapes. In fact, she could detect no color scheme at all.

"Grandmother's castoffs, relegated to the old guest house after Grandfather died and she decided to redo the house in purple," Steven explained, apparently reading Lila's mind.

"I like it," she said.

"I do too, especially after a few hours in that study. When I leave here, I swear I will never own or covet a purple thing of any kind."

"What about an eggplant?" she asked as he opened the higher shutters.

"Hate the things."

"Grapes? Plums? Violets?"

"I will neither eat the first two nor grow the latter."

"But I love violets," Lila said.

He turned to face her. "I may have to make an exception then. Would you like something cold to drink?"

"Yes." She sat down on a red chair by the window and resisted the urge to open the sketch pad and begin on the room itself. It was so cluttered and yet so tidy. She decided the cluttered part was Endora's doing and the tidy part was Steven's. What was that old phrase she'd read about boats? A place for everything and everything in its place?

Steven reentered the room, two glasses in hand. He was wearing a sheepish grin that Lila understood the minute she tasted what he'd given her.

"Grape juice!"

"It's all I have." He drank his glass down in one swallow, set the glass on a table, and said, "I have something I want to show you."

She put her glass aside too and followed him into his bedroom. This room was less crowded with furniture and was equally neat. The minute her eyes swept the walls she saw what he'd wanted her to see, and she crossed the room to stand before it immediately.

"Where did you get it?" Lila asked.

"I told you I read an article about your aunt and was quite taken with a certain painting. When I discovered it was so small, only eight-by-ten inches, I decided I had to have it. It took a while, but I finally tracked it down. You should see it on *Ariel,* hanging in the main cabin where the light from the porthole hits it. I brought it with me when I moved here and covered the spot where it hangs on the bulkhead with that photograph of the boat in Tahiti, the one you were admiring last night."

Lila nodded, speechless. The last she'd heard, *Girl on a Sand Dune* had been in a wealthy Bostonian's collection. She could hardly believe Steven owned it. The small canvas was aglow with golden light, the figure off to one side at one with the windblown saw grass. She stared at the tiny rendition of her own face, painted eight years before, and saw the uncertainty mixed with cockiness that went with the age.

"I've always loved this," Lila said. "Aunt Connie did two paintings that day, this one and a much larger one. She gave me the larger and sold this, and I always wished she'd done it the other way around. This is the better painting."

"You have the larger painting?" Steven asked, standing very close behind her.

"No. I did, but then I had to sell it after she . . .

died. No, don't worry, I'm not going to cry. I can't tell you how delighted I am that you have this and that someday it will sail around the world with you and *Ariel.*''

She felt his hands on her shoulders and the gentle pressure for her to turn. When she did, she found his gaze concentrated and compelling, drawing her closer till their lips met. Shocked, Lila pulled away, but his hand caressed the back of her neck, pulling her close again, and this time the kiss lasted.

''I shouldn't have done that,'' he said a minute later, stepping back, his gaze drilling into Lila.

''I'm glad you did.''

''It just . . . complicates things.''

''Does it, Steven?''

''Yes, it does. I can't help how I feel about you or how you feel about me, of course, but you have to admit that this isn't the right time for either one of us to become—er—attached.''

Lila couldn't believe she was capable of being so annoyed with someone she was so close to loving. ''I wouldn't lose sleep over one little kiss,'' she said breezily. ''It's no big deal, you know. We're not the heroine and hero of your grandmother's books; a kiss does not a future seal.''

He crossed his arms. ''Oh?''

''That's right. And if you'd like, I'll just pretend it never happened.''

''You could do that?''

''Easily.'' She walked out of the room, calling over

her shoulder, "Thanks for the cold drink. See you later." It wasn't until she closed the front door behind her that the full impact of the kiss hit and her knees felt like Jell-O.

Chapter Eight

Endora didn't show up for the afternoon sitting. It took Lila every ounce of willpower she possessed not to march across the hall and summon her, but she decided against it. Endora was a big girl. Instead, Lila worked on the background.

The gardening service had arrived during lunch, and the drone of the lawn mower as the driver circled the huge grass yard formed a buzzing backdrop. Lila was so intent on her work that she didn't hear the door open and wasn't aware anyone else was in the room until she heard a clatter. She looked up and found the maid, Kaye.

"I'm sorry I disturbed you," Kaye said, bending to pick up the marble chess pieces she'd apparently sent to the floor.

Lila stretched. "That's okay. It's time for a rest,

anyway.'' She cast her painting one dissatisfied look and turned to watch Kaye put the pieces back on the chessboard, her stout fingers amazingly deft.

Steven was right, Lila thought. It was difficult to reconcile this woman as a thief.

''You don't live here, do you?'' she asked.

Kaye straightened up slowly, pushing her limp brown hair behind her ears to keep it from swinging in her face. ''No, I live in town.''

''San Diego is such a pretty place.''

Kaye glanced at Lila through the corners of her eyes. ''Some of it is,'' she agreed.

''I saw Coronado last night,'' Lila said. ''From the water, that is. I thought it looked enchanting. But there's something about the water at night, isn't there?''

''It makes everything look all innocent,'' Kaye said softly, her dust rag floating over the low table, but her voice suddenly eager. ''It makes everything magical.''

Lila sat down on the edge of the sofa. She studied Kaye's blunt features, thinking to herself that there was nothing poetic about the face or figure of this woman, but her soul seemed touched with light. She looked into Kaye's eyes—no mean trick as Kaye tended to keep her gaze cast toward the floor, and she fancied she saw sprinkles of stardust in the brown depths.

''You do understand.''

Kaye smiled shyly. ''I don't live far from the water,'' she said. ''My husband and I have a small house a few miles away. Sometimes, at night, we drive down to the beach and walk a while. You know how it is. Gary says the lights look like fairy eyes. He's like that.''

"He sounds nice."

Kaye looked up suddenly, her mouth spreading into a smile. "Oh, he is nice. We've only been married a few months."

"Still honeymooners."

Kaye shrugged. She went back to dusting, and Lila scolded herself. Here she was so taken with a few fanciful words that she'd totally forgotten what Kaye was accused of doing. She said, idly, she hoped, "It's hard to make ends meet nowadays, isn't it? Even with two jobs it's a struggle."

"For a lot of people," Kaye agreed as she started dusting a ceramic lamp painted with lilacs. "Gary and I are lucky. His folks have a little house they were renting out, but when we got married, they insisted we use it. It sure helps."

Lila nodded, happy to hear it. In her mind, irrational as it might seem to someone else, Kaye was exonerated of all wrongdoing.

"Except for the doctor bills," Kaye added as a postscript.

"Doctor bills?"

"For my older brother. He was in a car accident a few days before Gary and I got married. Uninsured, of course. I hated saddling Gary with my brother's doctor bills, but Tim is the only family I have. Who will take care of him if I don't?"

Lila nodded again, well acquainted with that particular rationale.

"So we struggle to keep up just like everyone else," Kaye said, moving on to the curio cabinet. "I don't know what we'd do if I didn't have this job. Mrs. Yolette is a very nice woman. Anyway, when Tim gets better and the doctor bills stop, we'll be fine."

Lila nodded yet again; she was beginning to feel like one of those loose-headed dolls people used to fasten to the dashboards of their cars, the kind with the head mounted on a spring so that every time the car rolled over a bump, the head bobbed up and down.

"Every penny helps," Kaye added under her breath, reminding Lila of Aunt Connie's lawyer. Lila looked at Kaye again. Burdened with a recovering brother and a new marriage, it was possible even a seemingly decent woman like Kaye might be tempted to help herself to a little extra cash from the purse of an obviously well-to-do but forgetful boss. All Lila knew was that it wasn't any of her business, and she decided on the spot to drop all investigations. As far as she was concerned, a few dollars were better lost to Kaye than twice the amount to Jay! The morality of stealing would have to be up to someone else to figure out.

The only problem was that she'd mentioned the whole affair to Steven. Would he feel duty bound to question Kaye?

"Is something wrong, Miss Greene?"

Lila looked up quickly. "Oh, no, nothing."

"Your painting is pretty."

Kaye was standing in front of the incomplete portrait. "I've barely begun," Lila said. She was unhappy with the portrait, she realized suddenly. Very unhappy with it. The unhappiness grew exponentially by the second. The pose and dress were okay, but there was something missing, and suddenly Lila knew what it was.

She turned to find that Kaye had left the room. Lila walked through the open door and across the tiled entry and knocked softly on Endora's study door. No answer, but since the door was ajar and she heard Endora's voice booming from within, she nudged it open, and for a moment stood unobserved, watching and listening as Endora dictated quickly to Steven.

"Desdemona faced the wind, her long hair flying behind her, tears streaming down her cheeks. On the ground at her feet was her beloved Scout, the dog who had always been there during her turbulent youth, her oldest friend. An arrow shaft protruded from his chest, stilling the faithful heart. Surely this was the most bitter blow of all, but rather than destroying her, it strengthened her resolve, and she swore on her dead friend's memory that she would find the perpetrator of this dastardly deed and see that he, or she, paid for it. And after that? 'After that,' Desdemona shouted to the wind, 'I'll have things my way!' ''

"Did you get all that, Steven?" Endora asked.

"Yes, of course," he said without looking up. Lila thought to herself that he must take shorthand.

"It just seems to be pouring from me this time, as though it's already written in my head and can't wait to get out. Isn't it thrilling? Oh, I know, you don't really write like I do—you know, creatively—but surely you can see how easily this book is coming. Not like the first one you helped me with, my dear, where every word had to be yanked out of me and was forgotten almost as soon as I uttered it.''

"*Murder in Neon*?" Lila asked.

Both Endora and Steven turned to face the door.

"Oh, I'm sorry, I didn't mean to startle you. The door was open, and you didn't hear me knock, so I listened to a little of your book, Endora. It sounds thrilling."

Endora beamed. "Thank you, dear. It is thrilling."

"But the last book you wrote was *Murder in Neon,* right?"

"Yes," she said, studying her hands.

"I thought so. It was wonderful. I was on the edge of my chair the entire time. Actually, I read it in bed, so I guess I should say I was on the edge of my mattress." Lila thought to herself that she must stop babbling, but the other two people were so deathly quiet that she didn't know what to do. "You must be very proud of it," she finished lamely.

"Of course," Endora said.

Lila cleared her throat and looked at Steven, who was equally busy avoiding her eyes.

"You forgot to come sit for me," Lila finally said.

Endora looked up. "Is it that late? Oh, forgive me, child. I just got on a roll with the book and couldn't quit. We're very close to the end. Wouldn't you say so, Steven?"

"It seems so."

"Yes. Tomorrow we'll start with Desdemona go-

ing to church, where she can confront the three suspects—''

''Or perhaps she could plan a party,'' Steven interrupted softly. ''She could invite everyone in the book,
including the three suspects.''

''Oh, yes! That way they'll be at the house, and
when Mr. Smythe tries to get away, Robert Turnstone
can chase after him. I see a grand scene at night across
the moors—''

''On horseback?''

''Yes, as you say, on horseback. Desdemona can
take out after the two men and be the one to resolve
the conflict.''

''Sounds good to me,'' Steven said. ''You're brilliant, Endora.''

Endora actually blushed. ''Thank you, my dear.''

Lila sighed. ''Endora, this is all very exciting, but
we really must work on your portrait. Your party is
only four days away, and it would be nice if it was
finished, wouldn't it?''

''But my book. My agent is flying here from New
York for the party. We're great old friends, Fran and
I. Why, she was the first one to insist my heroines—''

''Excuse me, Grandmother,'' Steven interrupted,
''but Lila is trying to tell you you have to pose for her
tomorrow.''

''All in one sitting,'' Lila said on the impulse.

Endora looked shocked. ''What!''

''This is too disjointed. I'm going to stretch a new
canvas tonight and start all over tomorrow morning,
and neither one of us is going to move until the thing

is done. Steven can come in there and copy your words or use a tape recorder. I don't care what you do as long as I am allowed to proceed with what I do!''

Out of the corners of her eyes, she saw Steven's eyebrows shoot up his forehead. Endora said, ''I suppose if I must—''

''Good.'' Lila smiled at both of them and marched back across the hall to the drawing room, breathing in great lungfuls of non-lilac-scented air as she moved. One look at the portrait in progress reaffirmed her resolve, and for a second she empathized with the lovely Desdemona! She would have things her way. . . .

''Now, Jay, I simply insist!'' Endora said that night. ''We want to hear about your new job. And don't tell us you don't want to jinx it, because if you already have it, how could you?''

''I wouldn't want to bore you,'' Jay answered. All four of them were seated around the outside patio table because the weather was so mild and Cook had decreed a barbecue. He was a huge man, a fact that had escaped Lila's attention the first and only other time she'd seen him. Not particularly big around, but tall and formidable-looking. He didn't have a hair on his head, but his face and manner were gentle and, for living in the Sun Belt, his skin was incredibly pale.

If she were to paint him, she thought, she'd tint the white with just a few dabs of yellow ochre and cadmium red light. He was standing behind a haze of smoke as he basted the ribs with his secret sauce. Rose, perched on the brick bench to his right, looked on with interest.

"You won't bore us," Steven said. "On the contrary."

Jay cast his cousin an unpleasant look. "Just suffice it to say that I now work in an office."

"Oh, Jay!" Endora squealed. "How delightful!"

Lila thought it sounded dreadful, at least the way Jay said it. "Do you work with nice people?" she asked.

Jay stood abruptly. "Cook, is dinner about done? I have to go out tonight."

"Almost," Cook said. The aroma of the sizzling meat made Lila's mouth water. She took a sip of chilled white wine.

Jay looked down at her and apologized for not answering. "I work with very nice people," he told her, touching her cheek. "The office is modern, and the work is interesting." He looked at his grandmother and added, "Okay?"

"Of course, dear. What kind of an office?"

"A bank," he said.

"Oh, Steven, did you hear, a bank? Remember little Gilda? She worked at a bank too. She got that promotion and met the president of the bank, and a month later they were married!"

"Is Gilda a niece of yours?" Lila asked.

"A character in one of her books," Jay said dryly. He sat back down as Cook announced dinner was ready.

Later that night, after Endora had gone upstairs to

watch television and Jay had disappeared up the driveway in his car, Lila found herself alone. It was dark by this time, and the wind had come up, and as she stood at the top of the cliff, her skirt wrapped around her legs, she found her thoughts straying to Steven.

She thought of the painting of her that hung in his room and the coincidence that he should have gone to so much effort to secure it. And, of course, she thought about his kiss and and the feel of his strong arms around her back and his hands running through her hair. She closed her eyes and recreated him, only this time he told her he loved her instead of apologizing and ruining everything. What was he so afraid of?

"Me," Lila said out loud. She looked toward the trees. The tall giants rustled in the wind, and their pungent odor drifted across the yard. Lila saw lights and knew Steven was there, alone, like she was.

What would he do if she marched up to his door and knocked? What would he do if, upon opening his door, he found his arms full of a frustrated artist intent upon kissing him? She felt her feet move, and then she began running, the wind at her back, over the grass, into the forest, along the dirt path, ending up at the small house buried in the trees.

She caught her breath on the doorstep, her hand poised to knock, and then she saw the front window was open. She also became aware of a familiar sound. She craned her neck to look and found Steven, facing the window, sitting at a desk, his fingers tapping the keyboard of a small computer. She watched him for several minutes as her heartbeat gradually returned to normal and her hand dropped to her side. He didn't stop typing once, nor did he look up.

"Good night," she whispered and softly walked away from the small house and the man within.

By the next morning Lila had read another one of Endora's books, this one originally published twenty years before. She'd liked the book very much and, as Endora settled into the wicker chair, told her so.

"The people were so warm and likable," she said.

"I liked that one too," Endora agreed.

Lila had already stretched the canvas and set out her palette. She began working as Endora dictated Desdemona's fate to Steven, who had set up temporary shop in the corner of the room, his desk an oak TV tray. She hardly heard them speaking, and any distraction they caused was countered by the fact that Endora's face came alive as she unwound her story.

Lila found the spark that had been missing before—passion. Passion for work and ideas, for the very words Endora used the way Lila used paints. A healthy amount of it was reflected in Endora's face as she told her story; now the portrait began to paint itself as Lila worked feverishly to keep up with whatever it was that caused the brush to move this way or that with whatever color it automatically mixed on the palette.

She wasn't aware of time until she felt a hand on her shoulder and, pausing, discovered Steven looking down at her. "Time for a break?" he suggested.

"Hm—" Lila said as she added a touch of burnt sienna to mix the color of the shadow of Endora's chin on her neck.

"It's been three hours," Steven said softly. "Endora is exhausted."

Lila looked more closely at her subject's eyes.

"It's true, dear, I am," she confirmed.

Lila nodded. "Okay, take a three-hour break, but then back to work."

Endora stood stiffly. "Steven, be a love and tell Rose I'll eat my lunch upstairs, will you?"

"Okay."

Endora swept out of the room, regal-looking in her gown. Steven tapped Lila's shoulder again and said, "Come with me. We'll get Cook to make us a sandwich or something."

"No, thanks," Lila said, her attention already back on the painting. She'd replaced the silk lilacs with the real things this morning, barely intercepting an assault from Endora's can of air freshener. She mixed blue and red, added white—

"I'll see you later then," he said.

"Hm—" Lila answered as she began on the general form of the vase of flowers.

Steven reappeared an hour later with a tray. He set it down beside Lila, saluted when she finally noticed him, and left. She smiled as she saw half a turkey sandwich oozing with cranberry sauce, a sliced apple, a few cookies, and a big glass of milk. She took a deep breath and a couple of short turns around the room to clear her head and stretch her legs. The windows were wide open, and she looked toward the newly mown grass with a deep sense of regret that she would be leaving. It was such a beautiful estate.

With one last breath of spring air, she walked back to her easel, bumping into the TV tray as she passed and sending dozens of sheets of paper sailing to the floor. As she picked them up, she couldn't help but notice the papers that weren't blank were covered with script, not shorthand. For a second she wondered how she would get them back in the right order without taking the time to read them, but then she saw the carefully written page numbers in the right-hand corners.

It wasn't until she was restacking them that she discovered there were two of every number and, upon closer scrutiny, that each numbered sequence was for a different story. On top, she put the one in which the name Desdemona jumped out—it was also the most neatly written manuscript, as the other was heavily edited with crossed-out lines and inserted words—and went back to work. As she painted in the legs of the glass table, making sure they faded into the background until they disappeared, she munched on the cookies.

Endora was prompt, and Lila went back to work on her face. Steven read back the last few pages of Endora's book because Endora insisted she needed to find the same ''voice,'' and Lila began to see more parallels between her work and Endora's work. Pretty soon she was caught in the magic of her creation, and every outside distraction was nonexistent.

''Never fuss with hair,'' Aunt Connie had told her years before. Lila had already mixed the dark tones and painted them in, then the light tones. Now she painted in the general shape of the disciplined wave in

Endora's hair and indicated the various lights. Using a dry brush, she blended the edges into the background.

Details now, she told herself, and began refining shapes and colors. She reshaped the contours of the cheekbone, warmed some of the halftones, added dark shadows to the eye sockets, and mixed ultramarine blue for the irises. Her brush danced over Endora's dress and fluttered above the lilacs, barely touching the canvas.

It was almost finished. Today the beauty mark had climbed high on Endora's right cheek, practically under the far corner of her eye. Lila painted it in.

She stood back, her arms and shoulders stiff. She looked from the painting to the model and knew in a sudden blinding moment of insight that Endora's portrait was the finest work she'd done to date. She could see traces of her aunt's style, but there was a definite stamp of her own there too, and she smiled with the pleasure of having put in a good day's work.

"Are you finished?" Endora asked.

"More or less," Lila said, adding the sparkle to the diamonds on the hands.

"May we see?" Steven asked.

Lila nodded. "Go stand by your grandmother, and I'll turn the easel so you can both see at once," she said. When they were in place, Lila carefully turned the painting.

"Oh!" Endora cried. "Oh, Lila darling!"

Lila smiled at Endora, but her gaze strayed to Steven, and the respect she saw in his returned gaze meant more than she ever would have anticipated.

"Is it always like that?" he asked.

"No," she said, knowing he understood that what had happened between her and the canvas was special this time. She was inordinately pleased he hadn't seen her struggle with one of Aunt Connie's board of directors portraits.

"Lila," Endora said after further inspection. "My beauty mark. Isn't it a little close to my eye?"

Lila thought to herself: *diplomacy*. For the life of her she didn't know exactly what to say.

Steven said, "Just a moment." He disappeared out the door and reappeared almost at once with a small wall mirror surrounded with seashells that Lila had noticed hanging next to the front door. He held it up to Endora. "Now what do you think, Grandmother?"

She looked at her reflection, then at Lila's portrait. "You're right. Such a clever boy. Lila dear, you made me look beautiful."

"You are beautiful," Lila said. "And I can change the position of the beauty mark if you wish."

"No, thanks, dear. I really shouldn't be saying this, but I seldom get the silly thing on the same place twice in a row." She followed this disclosure with a gusty roar of laughter. Lila suspected Endora's laughter was half pleasure and half relief that the whole thing was over. "Steven, will you help Lila pick up or whatever it is she has to do? I'm going to go find Rose and talk her into heating me a bowl of mushroom soup and feeding it to me in my own bed tonight."

After she'd left, Steven helped Lila put the easel in an out-of-the-way corner. Together they carried the palette and dirty brushes out to the garage, where Steven insisted he'd clean them while she finished in the drawing room. Lila was shocked to see how late it was—the sun was almost on the horizon.

After a shower she walked outside. It was dark by this time, but the patio was lit by several small lanterns. She saw candles on the table and a champagne bucket with a foil-wrapped bottle top peeking from beneath a cloth napkin. Soft music was coming from a portable tape recorder. Steven was sitting at the table, but when he saw Lila, he stood and in a few steps was beside her.

"I cooked you dinner," he said. He was dressed casually, as usual, his cotton shirt and pants setting off his bronze skin and the gold highlights in his hair.

"You?"

"Who do you think cooks aboard *Ariel*?"

"The captain, I take it. But when did you have time to cook?"

"While you worked during lunch. I made spinach crepes and filled them with lox topped with Swiss cheese— Well, you'll have to taste it to believe it. I hope."

"Where's Cook?"

"Night off. Endora had to bribe him with Thursday night to get him to stay here Sunday and cook for her party. And before you ask, Rose has retired to her own rooms, Endora is asleep, and Jay is—I don't know where Jay is."

"So it's just you and me?"

Steven had been opening the wine as he spoke. He

handed Lila a half-full glass and clicked his against hers. "It's just you and me."

"Aren't you afraid that what with the champagne and the music and soft, warm air you might be tempted to kiss me, causing the world as we know it to fall apart?"

"I'm willing to chance it," he said.

They put their glasses down and began dancing. Lila was determined to keep her head, but it was awfully tempting to melt against Steven and operate on instincts alone.

They ate dinner, which was as good as he promised it would be; then they danced some more. Steven kissed Lila once or twice, but with restraint. It was almost as though he were determined to stay away from her and at the same time powerless to do so. Lila found the old questions resurfacing in her mind. Questions like, why didn't he let Endora hire another secretary and get on with his life, and why was he so critical of his cousin? And, most of all, why did he hold back with her? All these questions were on the tip of her tongue, but she kept them there, sensing the time to speak wasn't right.

She kissed his chin and, when he looked down, kissed his mouth. She longed to whisper, "I love you," but had the instinct he'd bolt if she did. Instead, she said, "It's getting a little chilly. I think I'll go up to bed."

"Wait," he said, tucking her hand against his chest. "Lila, what are you going to do next?"

"You mean now that I've finished Endora's portrait? Well, after her party I guess I'll leave."

"And go where?"

"I don't know, Steven. At least I have a little money now, enough to sustain me while I look for a job. I owe your grandmother a lot for that."

"She's the one in debt," he said, his grip around Lila's hand tightening. "You created something wonderful today, you know."

"Do you think so?"

"I do. I'm in awe of your talent."

Lila didn't answer.

"You have to nurture it," he said. "You have to figure out a direction and pursue it with determination."

"Like you?" Lila asked and was instantly sorry she'd spoken.

His grip loosened, but still he held her. "I can't tell you what I'd need to tell you to make you understand," he said after an interminable pause. "You're right—I did abandon my dream. I traded it in, I guess, and I don't know how long I'll be stuck with it. But you're not like me, Lila. My dreams are selfish pursuits. *Ariel* is just a boat, and I have the rest of my life to sail her around the world. Your talent is world-class."

"Oh, I'll continue painting," she told him. "There's nothing in the world that could change that. It's not something I can control; it's there. It's part of me."

"Most people would say that, to an artist, art is everything," he said. "Like it was for your aunt."

"Hm—" She looked into Steven's eyes, and something in her head clicked. She saw him typing at the computer, sitting behind his pile of papers while Endora rattled on, walking through the trees of an evening. She said, ''It's just occurred to me that you and I are a lot alike.''

''Not me,'' he insisted. ''I don't have a talent like yours.''

''That's hogwash, and I suspect you know it,'' Lila answered softly and, kissing Steven on his baffled lips, slipped out of his arms and into the house.

Before climbing the stairs, she went into the study and turned on a light. Kneeling, she scanned the titles, disappointed when she didn't find what she was looking for. She stood up and hastily searched the top of Endora's desk. Foiled again, she looked on the only other accessible place—Steven's desk. There it was, beneath three manila folders. She picked it up, and with a sense of unreality saw what she had suspected but was still shocked to find. She took the book up the stairs with her, and by the middle of the night had begun to figure out some of the answers to her questions.

Chapter Nine

LILA awoke with a start, instantly alert. She had to make herself take a shower and put on shorts and a cotton shirt before dashing down the stairs. How many times had she slept on a painting and awakened to find it half as good as she'd thought it was? Too many times to be complacent now.

She threw open the door to Endora's drawing room, and there it was, just as she'd left it the evening before. She smiled slowly and took a very deep breath, noticing for the first time that the tile floors were cool on her bare feet and water from her hair was soaking into the collar of her shirt.

"Happy?"

Lila twirled to find Jay, coffee mug in hand, standing behind her. He was dressed in a gray suit and looked every inch the handsome banker. He slipped a slim wallet into his inside breast pocket as he took a couple of steps toward Lila.

"Yes," she said.

"I don't blame you. You did what I said couldn't be done." He stole a glance over his shoulder toward the stairs and added, "You made Endora look good."

"It wasn't hard," Lila said defensively. "You must realize how unique your grandmother is, Jay."

He shrugged and glanced at his watch. "I've got to go," he said. He picked up a briefcase he'd deposited by the door, and Lila moved to the window to watch him drive away, one hand on the wheel, one hand still clutching the mug. Well, at least he was working.

"You're up bright and early," Steven said.

Again Lila twirled around. Steven was dressed in shorts and an exotically colorful T-shirt. He looked tired, but there was some other expression on his face that seemed to override the fatigue.

"I had to see the painting," she explained.

"To make sure it's as good as you remembered it being," he said.

Lila nodded. "Where's Endora?"

"Still in bed. As a matter of fact, she sent Rose to tell me that she's going to take a day off today and spend her time resting. Her big party is the day after tomorrow, you know."

"And I tired her out yesterday."

"She wanted her portrait done by a professional, and she got it. Meanwhile I have the day off, and so do you."

Lila smiled. "Don't you have to closet yourself out in your little house and type Endora's manuscript?"

He returned her smug smile with an equally smug smile of his own. "Not today. I need to buy Endora a birthday present. Why don't you come along with me? I'll treat you to a great Mexican lunch in the old part of town."

"Margaritas too?"

"If you insist."

"I insist. How are you dressing for this excursion?"

"Just like this," he said, "except I'll probably put on a pair of shoes."

"Fifteen minutes?"

"Fifteen minutes."

Actually, it was more like an hour before they met again in the front hall. During that time Kaye had come and was busy mopping the tile floor, so they tiptoed around the edges and made their way outside.

"We'll have to take Grandmother's car," Steven explained as he opened the passenger door of a beautifully kept 1967 aqua Chrysler with a white roof. "I sold mine up in Seattle."

"It's neat, isn't it?"

"You just wait." Sure enough, once he'd backed it out into the driveway, he pushed a button, and the top began to fold into the back.

"You may not believe this, but I've never ridden in a convertible before!" Lila said as they breezed along, the wind snapping their hair. She laughed with pleasure and looked at Steven, who grinned at her, and she knew, *she knew,* she wasn't leaving Endora's house without somehow rescuing Steven from himself.

He took Lila to a charming restaurant across from an old church and graveyard. While he ordered, Lila watched several women make tortillas, their hands nimble and quick. They ate a huge lunch, drank tart margaritas, then, hand in hand, walked along the sidewalk. Lila felt exactly like a tourist, but she didn't mind one bit. It was the first time in two years she'd wandered aimlessly along without knowing that the time of relative freedom would soon come to a screeching halt. The ugly truth was that Aunt Connie's death had been long and difficult and painful, but not just for Aunt Connie. Lila felt like a person who had been ill and was now recovering.

"In here," Steven said suddenly, gesturing toward a doorway off to their right. It was a jewelry store, and while Steven looked in the cases, Lila studied the original watercolors hanging on the wall. Some of them were quite nice, and she wondered if she shouldn't try using them again sometime. That and acrylics, she mused. She was tired of the solvents needed for oils and would have switched long ago if it hadn't been for Aunt Connie's reluctance to change. As a matter of fact, she remembered suddenly, she even had a box of them in her trunk.

"Lila, what do you think of this?" He held up a giant amethyst dangling from a gold chain.

"Good grief, it's huge!"

"Five carats," Steven said.

"Endora will love it."

"The bigger the better, huh? That's what I thought." He told the clerk he'd take it. While he completed the transaction, Lila wandered out to the sidewalk and looked in the window of the shop next door. She ducked her head back in the jewelry store and said, "Meet you in front of the church in half an hour?"

"Sure," Steven said.

Lila went into the shop, bought the dress she'd spied in the window, and went to meet Steven.

"Would you mind dropping by *Ariel*?" he asked as they got back into the car.

"Of course not." She settled into her seat and drank in the warm air as they drove the city streets back toward the water.

In the daylight *Ariel*, with her varnished cabin and ample beam, took Lila's breath away. Her masts were tall and straight, her decks wide, her cockpit so picture perfect it reminded Lila of a miniature movie set. She was enchanted, and as Steven dug around inside for whatever it was he needed, she took off her shoes, sat behind the wheel, and pretended she was taking *Ariel* through a coral reef somewhere in the South Pacific.

"Catch," Steven said. Lila looked up in time to see a blur of white sailing her way. One-handed, she caught the baseball cap and tugged it on her head. Her eyes shaded, she called out her thanks to Steven, who grinned before disappearing back inside the cabin.

Later they walked up the dock, Steven toting *Ariel's* genoa jib stuffed into a blue sail bag because he claimed it needed to be taken home and checked for wear. Lila looked up when she heard a motor beating and found

Donna Ransom on the foredeck of a huge motorboat. The yacht was slowly approaching the dock, and Donna held a coiled line. Steven dropped his sail in the middle of the dock and moved to the side of the slip they were aiming for to catch the line when Donna threw it. Lila admired Steven's back and shoulders as he wrapped the line around a dock cleat, then moved down the finger to catch the aft line.

"Beautiful afternoon for a sail," Lila said.

Donna looked over her shoulder toward the stern. "Yeah," she said, glancing back, smiling nervously.

When Donna looked aft again, Lila's gaze followed. She saw Steven standing on the dock with a line in his hand. He said something to the man in the stern of the boat, a man Lila couldn't see; then he threw the line down and walked toward Lila.

"Steve," Donna pleaded.

Steven caught Lila's elbow and propelled her forward as he effortlessly hefted the sail bag and propped it on top of his shoulder. For one awful moment Lila wondered if Steven was jealous that Donna had had the boat out with another man; then she recalled his kisses the night before, and she suspected those concerns were unfounded. "What in the world—" she began as they climbed the ramp toward the parking lot.

"Nothing," he snapped.

Lila heard footsteps behind them and, twisting around, was surprised to see Jay running toward them.

"Steven!" Lila said.

He ignored her.

Jay caught up with them at the top of the ramp. "Steve—"

"I have nothing to say to you," Steven said.

Lila yanked her arm free. "Stop hauling me around!" she told Steven. Then, turning to face Jay, she added, "What are you doing here? I thought you were working at a bank."

Jay ignored Lila and searched his cousin's face. "Are you going to tell her?"

"Why shouldn't I?" Steven barked. "You lied to her. You never even applied for a job, much less got one, did you? You're using her, and you know it."

"Aren't you doing the same thing?" Jay yelled.

"No, I am not doing the same thing."

"Boys, boys," Lila attempted to say, but Jay's voice was louder than hers.

"Then what do you call it? She feeds you and houses you, and all you do is perform the same duties some secretary could perform. You gave up your boat and everything else you cared about just to live off Grandmother, and if that isn't using her, I don't know what is."

"Jay, you don't know what you're talking about," Lila said.

Steven turned his attention to Lila. She could see he was wondering how much she knew, and she could also see that he was praying she'd keep it to herself. She sighed heavily.

"And what about Endora's money?" Jay continued. Lila suspected guilt was putting him on the offensive. He was so upset, he didn't see the dangerous narrowing of Steven's eyes. "You have both hands in her finances—don't think I don't know that. You could be bleeding her dry, and she wouldn't have the slightest idea."

"None of this is your concern," Steven said ominously.

"Don't forget, half of what that woman owns is mine."

"And don't you forget that I am aware of what happened to her checks. You don't forge her signature very well, Jay. I closed the account before you could do more harm, but now I hear money is disappearing from Grandmother's purse, and I don't believe for one moment that Kaye is responsible. I covered for you before because she loves you. I didn't want to upset her, especially before her birthday, but this time you've gone too far."

Jay's challenging expression folded in on itself. "You . . . you won't tell her," he said. "Please—"

"Not if you leave," Steven said. "Soon."

"But—"

"No. You're thirty-two years old. Time you grew up."

"But Grandmother's inheritance—"

"In case you've forgotten, Jay, our grandmother is still very much alive and kicking."

Jay looked down at his feet.

Steven took Lila's hand. "Shall we go?" he asked.

"Yes," she mumbled, and with one last look at Jay's defeated form followed Steven to the car.

They didn't say much for the first half of the ride

home. Lila could imagine the jumble in Steven's mind, and for herself, she was putting substance to the words she'd heard exchanged. So Jay had stolen Endora's checks and had even forged one. Steven had known about it because he'd taken over Endora's finances, so he'd closed the account. He hadn't told, but no wonder he kept his eye on Jay and had very few good things to say about his charming cousin! Was Jay really stealing from Endora, though?

"I'm very sorry," Steven said.

Lila put her hand on his. "It's okay. I don't blame you for being angry."

"What I meant was that I'm sorry I dragged you up the dock like that. It was rude and presumptuous of me. It's just that I lost my head when I saw Jay, and I knew if I didn't escape from him, I'd punch him in the nose."

Lila, thinking of poetic justice, wished he had.

"He's going to have to leave now," Steven continued. "That, at least, is good."

"And then will you leave?" Lila asked.

He spared her a quick glance as he guided the car up the hill. "No, I can't leave yet. I wish I could explain, Lila. Your opinion of me counts—"

"How long have you been writing Endora's books?" Lila interrupted.

This time the look he spared her was so long, she had to remind him to watch the road. She saw him swallow as he directed his attention to driving, but at the first turn-out, he pulled off the road and switched off the engine. He rested his forehead against the steering wheel for a second; then he looked at Lila from beneath his arm. "How did you find out?" he asked.

Lila laughed softly. "I think I suspected something for quite a while. I assumed you were taking her dictation in shorthand—I mean, how else could you have kept up with her? Yesterday, when I saw your notes were written in longhand—neatly, I might add, while another manuscript looked the way I figured a manuscript in progression would actually look, I really got curious. To tie things up, I found one of Endora's books on your desk last night. Its title is *Call of the Wind*, and it was written thirty years ago. I read it, Steven. It's the same exact book Endora is currently dictating to you."

He cast her a wary look and sighed deeply.

"Amazing how Desdemona trips Mr. Smythe as he runs along the moors so that by the time Robert Turnstone arrives on the scene, she's sitting on the villain's back, holding his own knife against his neck. Who would have thought little Desdemona had it in her! I suppose finding her dog Scout dead—"

"That's enough," Steven said. He dropped his hand and stared at Lila without, she supposed, really seeing her. Finally he said, "Last year, after the secretary quit and I started taking Endora's dictation, I discovered just how out of whack with things she really was. She dictated a book to me, all right, but it didn't make any sense. So I started working on it myself—you know, fixing it up.

"Every morning when she'd ask me to reread what she'd written the day before, I'd read her what I'd done to it during the night. She liked what she heard, but by the time we finished it, there wasn't much resemblance between her words and *Murder in Neon*. However, she accepted it, mainly, I think, because her agent loved it. The book just came out, and it's doing well.''

''I read it,'' Lila reminded him. ''I thought it was fantastic, and in my heart I think I knew from the very beginning that you wrote it.''

''Thank you.''

''So why didn't you do it again with this book?''

''You've seen the way Endora's face clouds over when you mention *Murder in Neon*. Somewhere in the back of her mind, she knows she didn't really write it. I just didn't have the heart to deceive her again.'' He looked away from Lila and added, ''Besides, the characters and plot of *Call of the Wind* made the possibility of pulling something like that off twice in a row almost impossible.''

''Because Endora knew the plot and characters too well,'' Lila said softly.

''Considering she first wrote it three decades ago, it's incredible how well she remembers it. After the first few chapters, I thought it sounded familiar, so I looked and, sure enough, there it was on her shelf. It even has the same title.''

''So every night you write out a chapter or so of *Call of the Wind*, and every morning you pretend you're copying what she says when you're actually working on another book.''

He nodded.

''Is your second book any good?''

"I think so," he said. "I finished it last night. I named the characters the same as Endora's characters, but a gun-toting Desdemona leaves something to be desired. There's no way in the world she's going to be fooled by it this time."

"Oh, Steven."

"If I tell her, it'll break her heart, maybe even her spirit. If I don't, I'm stuck here developing a real love for something I can't even claim as my own. And add to that the fact that she's almost finished. What happens when she sends in that manuscript? At first I tried to write a parallel story, hoping I could convince her to let me do some major revisions that would result in my book, but things being as they are with writing, my story took over until it no more resembles Desdemona's Victorian plight than it does Mother Goose. So there you have it. My duplicity is going to hurt the very one I was trying to shield, probably more than knowledge of Jay's stealing would."

Lila stared out at the horizon. It seemed impossible that she'd only been here a few days, had known this man less than a week. She scooted close and said, "That's why you hold back with me."

He looked down at her and touched her cheek with gentle fingers. "No, my darling, that has nothing to do with it. I hold back with you for your sake, not mine."

"What?"

"You've just spent two years caring for your aunt. I wouldn't dream of tying you down again. I meant what I said about your talent. I won't stand in the way of your future.''

''I wish you'd stop worrying about my future,'' she said. ''I'm not a little kid who needs parental guidance.''

''I know you're not a little kid,'' he said slowly, his eyes delving into hers. ''Believe me, I know it.''

''So what's so awful about us falling in love?''

He sighed and, averting his gaze, said, ''When Endora finds out what I've done, I doubt she'll ever want to see my face again.''

''You'll be free to leave. You'll be free to sail *Ariel* around the world.''

He nodded. ''If I delay it a second time, I'll never go—''

''But *Ariel* is a big boat, Steven. There's room for two aboard her, isn't there?''

He touched her cheek with longing fingers. ''Of course. In a minute. But what kind of career could you build that way? No, like I said before, the fact is that falling in love will do neither one of us a bit of good. Our timing stinks.''

''Will you let me take care of me?'' she asked, a little annoyed.

''I know what you've been doing for the last two years,'' he said, ''and I think it proves that you're not very good at looking out for your own interests. Your heart is too big.''

''You have a lot of nerve talking to me like this,'' she said. ''We're peas in a pod.''

He opened his mouth to protest, but Lila effectively

cut him short by firmly planting her lips over his. As the sun dipped toward the horizon, Steven pulled the car back into the traffic and resumed the journey home.

"At least we beat Jay," Steven said as he drove the big Chrysler into the garage. It had been a quiet drive, both of them lost in unhappy thoughts.

"I don't imagine he's too anxious to get here," Lila pointed out. "Who does that car belong to?" She was referring to a small white sports car that had pulled up in the driveway next to her own red compact.

"I haven't the slightest idea," he said.

Steven left Lila on the front patio, explaining he was going out to the guest house to spread the sail out on the floor. Lila walked in the front door, restless and uneasy. She knew Steven's anxieties were valid ones. Maybe it was better to nip this attraction in the bud before either one of them ended up permanently ruined by it.

"Lila? Is that you, dear?"

"Just a moment, Endora," Lila called.

"There's someone I'm anxious for you to meet."

Lila dropped the sack with her dress in it on the bottom stair and detoured into the drawing room. The first thing she saw was her painting; the second, a man's back. He was wearing a tan suit and was studying the portrait. Even before he turned around, Lila saw something else that made her inhale sharply.

"Where did you get these?" she cried as she rushed into the room. Her drawings were everywhere, scattered on the floor, the tables, even the back of the sofa.

Endora said, ''Why, they were in your room on the dresser. I didn't think you'd mind—''

Lila hastily gathered her work and stacked it. She felt as though she'd been violated, as though her privacy had been breached. She was so caught up in reclaiming her work that she didn't hear Endora until the older woman said her name sharply.

''Lila!''

Lila looked up.

Endora said, ''This is Mr. Edward Booker, dear. I believe I told you he's the publisher of *Art Today*.''

Lila looked at Edward Booker. He was a tall man with salt-and-pepper hair and a trim beard. He returned her gaze with dark eyes behind horn-rimmed glasses. Lila thought he was probably in his mid-fifties, and try as she might, she could not recall meeting him before, though she knew she had. She accepted his hand and said, ''How are you?''

''Very well, thank you,'' he said, taking off his glasses and folding them into his pocket. ''You've changed a bit since last we met. I wouldn't have recognized you as the knock-kneed little girl Constance adored.''

''You've already met each other,'' Endora said, her purple lips pursed together in a pout.

''A long time ago,'' Lila said.

''Twelve or thirteen years,'' he agreed.

''He was a . . . a friend of my aunt's.'' Lila hadn't meant to pause over the word *friend,* but Edward showed no outward sign of noticing it.

''Yes,'' he said simply. ''Lila, I've been in Europe

for the last two months. When I got home last week, I found Endora's invitation in my mail. I came early, hoping Constance would be here. It wasn't until an hour ago that I found out she died. I knew she was sick, of course, but I didn't know it was—over.''

''Or that I'd painted Endora's portrait.''

''I knew that the minute I saw it,'' he said. ''Or rather, I knew she hadn't painted it.''

Lila cleared her throat. ''I see.''

''Do you? I meant that as a compliment to you.''

For a moment Lila forgot that Endora was still in the room and that she was a guest. All she could think of was the implied criticism. ''You were never fair to her,'' she said angrily. ''You let personal feelings interfere with your so-called professionalism.''

''On the contrary,'' he said stiffly. ''I greatly admired her early work, which yours is faintly reminiscent of. I did her a favor by ignoring her later work. Now, you show promise—''

''Constance Greene was twice the painter I will ever be, and you know it,'' Lila snapped. ''But you're right in one way. Keeping her name out of that pretentious magazine you publish couldn't have done anything but enhance her career!'' She turned on her heels and was horrified to see Endora's bewildered face.

Fleeing the room, she managed to hold bitter tears until she was alone, but once they came, they came in such a torrent that Lila was left weak and confused, certain that Edward Booker's long-standing snub of her aunt couldn't have caused such a flood of emotion.

It was a culmination, she decided as she showered, of a beautiful day wrecked first by Jay and then Edward.

And to top matters off, she thought as she furiously toweled herself dry until her skin was bright pink, she hadn't even managed to tell Endora how angry she was to have had her room invaded and her drawings taken downstairs to show to the likes of Edward Booker!

Dinner that night was as strained an event as Lila had ever attended. Jay sat across from her, refusing to meet her eyes. Edward sat beside Jay, and he, too, refused to look at Lila. Steven sat at one end of the table and picked at his food, casting annoyed glances at his cousin and longing looks at Lila. Rose served the dinner sullenly, especially around Jay, and Lila, ashamed of her outburst, tried hard not to look at anyone. Only Endora seemed oblivious to the tensions at the table and rattled on and on about something; Lila couldn't concentrate long enough to tell what it was she was talking about. It was a relief when Jay got up, threw his napkin down on his chair, and said, "I'm going out."

"Youth," Endora said to no one in particular.

Edward stood too. "If you'll excuse me, Endora, I believe I'll take a stroll around your magnificent yard."

"Yes, yes, go on," Endora said. After he'd left, she looked at Lila. "Are you all right?" she asked.

"I'm just so sorry," Lila admitted.

"I had no idea you and Edward Booker had ever met," she said. "And the fireworks!"

Lila looked at her. "It's a long story, Endora. I came

unglued when he made that snide comment about my aunt's work, but I shouldn't have thrown my temper tantrum in your house right in front of you. I'm very, very sorry.''

''Enough apologizing!'' Endora said.

''Is either one of you going to tell me what you're talking about?'' Steven asked.

In unison Endora and Lila said, ''No.''

''I see.''

Endora took a deep breath. ''Well, children, tomorrow is my eighty-sixth birthday. The day can't help but be better than today.''

''What does that mean?'' Steven asked.

''She means I upset her with my outburst,'' Lila explained.

''Oh, fiddle-faddle!'' Endora cried. ''That was nothing.''

''Then what do you mean?'' Lila asked.

Endora's eyes glowed. She might be upset, Lila thought fondly, but she did love an attentive audience.

''Well, first, I found I was missing more money out of my purse. I left it downstairs this morning, and by the time I got up and found it, Kaye was here, mopping the floor not ten feet from my purse. How she had the nerve to rob me and then stand there while I discovered it, I'll never know. She took over a hundred dollars!''

Lila and Steven exchanged meaningful glances. Steven asked, ''Did you actually see her steal the money?''

''Of course not, but who else would have robbed me in my own home?''

Lila thought of Jay that morning and the way she'd

seen him slip his wallet into his pocket as they spoke. Even if she didn't know what she did thanks to that illuminating fight at the Yacht Club, she would have suspected him.

"What did Kaye say?" Steven asked softly.

"She denied it. I fired her, anyway, of course. You should have heard her carrying on about her brother or something. I felt bad, but I can't have people stealing from me, can I, especially if she's going to be so brazen about it? I do have a right to protect myself, don't I?"

"Yes," Steven said, his voice equally anguished. "Of course you do. What else happened today?"

"Oh, let's see. Jay talked to me before dinner. He told me he's leaving the day after my party, that his new job demands he transfer to Los Angeles. He's only had that job a couple of days, Steven. What if he doesn't like it and wants to quit? He doesn't know anyone in Los Angeles."

"Grandmother, Los Angeles is hardly at the end of the earth. It's at most a couple of hours north of here. Besides, remember, Jay is older than I am. He can take care of himself."

"You just seem so much more competent," Endora said, her eyes shining with tears.

Lila could hardly stand holding her tongue. To see Endora shedding tears over Jay after he indirectly got Kaye fired was too much. She trusted Steven to do the right thing at the right time, however, so she kept silent.

"Let me see what I can do about . . . things," Steven said at last.

"Will you, dear?"

"Of course."

"I know I depend on you too heavily—"

"Now, Endora—"

"But I do! I know I do. Rose says I do. But don't you worry, darling. I have a surprise for you tomorrow, you'll see."

"It's your birthday," Steven said. "Tomorrow is your day to be surprised."

Endora smiled, but her eyes looked crafty, and suddenly Lila remembered the word *surprise* on the invitations and speculated on whether it was ever going to occur to Steven to wonder what his grandmother meant by it.

Chapter Ten

LILA waited until she was pretty sure Edward Booker was finished strolling around the yard before walking out toward the bluff in what had become a nightly ritual for her. Her mind cluttered with thoughts, she stood close to the edge and closed her eyes. Steven was in the drawing room, making small talk with Endora and probably Booker. Lila suspected his real motive was to keep an eye open for Jay's return. Kaye's unfair firing had changed things—Jay would have to admit taking the money. But would he? And if he didn't, did that leave it to Steven to have to break this news to Endora? How he must dread that prospect!

Steven. His very name made her glow from within and scowl from without, for she was discovering he was a man she couldn't easily put out of her mind. She remembered the afternoon at the beach below, his carefree laugh and sun-browned skin, his reluctance to talk about himself. Now she knew why.

Now she knew it was just too painful for him to discuss plans put on hold; he was obviously dying to sail *Ariel* away from San Diego, and yet he stayed because of Endora. Once that was over—as it was bound to be when Endora learned the truth about her last two books—he'd be free. Lila opened her eyes and felt tears slide down her cheeks. He'd be free unless he was in love with her and felt duty bound to stay. She would not be another anchor for him!

Yet, how could she pursue her own career while sailing around on a boat? That's what he'd been trying to say that afternoon—stay smart. Don't fall in love and begin another cycle of sacrifices.

"Lila?"

The voice was soft, so it didn't startle her. She turned and, thanks to the soft light cast by the patio lanterns, saw Edward Booker standing close behind her. "May I join you?" he asked.

Lila was about to say no when he added, "Please?"

"If you'd like."

He came and stood beside her, his gaze directed toward the faint white line of breaking waves far below. Lila felt tense with him standing so close, but at least she wasn't tempted to push him down the cliff as she would have been a few hours earlier.

"I owe Constance an apology," he said at last.

"Yes, you do. However, it's a little too late now."

"You don't understand," he said woodenly. "I . . . I loved your aunt. I worshiped the ground she walked on. When she refused me, she just about destroyed me. You're far too young to understand exactly what I'm talking about.''

"Maybe not," Lila said halfway to herself.

"It got so I couldn't bear to hear her name mentioned. We shared the same world in many ways, and our paths were always crossing. She was unflaggingly kind and professional.''

"So, for her kindness, you ignored her contributions and grew to hate her work? If that's the way you love, Booker—''

"I know. But I kept her out of the magazine because I knew I couldn't be impartial. You're right, though; the more she understood, the angrier I became. When I heard she was dying, I couldn't even bring myself to go see her. That's why Endora's invitation with the bold announcement that Constance was the artist of her portrait brought me here so fast.

"I hoped maybe I'd have a last chance to see her, to talk. . . . When I discovered she was dead, I felt twice betrayed, and your work was sitting there, reminding me of hers. And then in you walked and, merciful heavens, you look exactly like she did twenty years ago when she was your age. It was too much for me. I retreated into my comfortable old bitter coat and lashed out. I'm sorry, Lila. I can't tell Constance, but I can tell you. I truly am sorry.''

Lila looked at him. She saw the glisten of tears on his cheeks. She said, "Okay, Edward. I know Aunt Connie would have said something witty and clever and gotten you to laugh; all I can say is that I know she would have wanted you to forgive yourself and for you and me not to squabble. We both loved her in our own ways.''

She felt his hand take hers. ''Thank you, Lila.''

They stood like that for a while. Lila thought of Aunt Connie's decision to stay unmarried. She would never know if her aunt had loved Edward Booker, but she did know this: If she had, she'd goofed. She should have grabbed him and held on to him. It might sound corny, but she was beginning to understand that true love was worth more than all the paintings in the world, and anyway, how could love not improve the core of a human and, hence, her talent? Aunt Connie had been extremely selfish with her time; it had suited her. Or, Lila amended, perhaps she'd just never really loved someone enough.

The way she loved Steven?

''Shall we go inside and show Endora we can behave?'' Edward asked.

''Good idea but, knowing Endora, she'll probably be disappointed,'' Lila said as they walked back to the house.

Endora, whose eyebrows rose as Lila preceded Edward into the drawing room, smiled warmly at the obviously friendly duo. ''You two are talking again. Good. Edward, you rascal, come sit here by me. Lila, if you're searching the shadows for Steven, he isn't here. He went outside a few minutes ago. I'm surprised you didn't bump into each other.''

''We came in the back way,'' Lila said. ''I guess he went around the front.''

"Yes, he did. We heard a car, and I said something about Jay being back early, and he excused himself." Endora looked at Lila and winked broadly, her subtle way of reminding Lila that Steven was going to try to talk Jay out of moving to Los Angeles with his fictional job. If she only knew! Lila smiled noncommittally in return.

"Edward," Endora continued, "you do know Fran Crane, my agent, don't you?"

"Didn't I meet her at that party you threw in La Paz a few years back?"

"That's right. Her plane arrives in a couple of hours. Will you be an angel on wheels and go into town and meet it for me? I'd ask Steven or Jay, but both boys are acting so strange tonight."

"Excuse me," Lila said and left as Edward assured Endora he'd be delighted to meet Endora's agent's plane. She opened the front door and saw Jay sitting on the edge of the brick patio next to the moon-faded marigolds.

"Come on out here," Jay said when he saw her hesitate. "I won't bite."

Lila closed the door behind her and sat down beside Jay. He took her hand in both of his. "Do you hate me?" he asked.

"Of course not," Lila said immediately and was rewarded with a dazzling smile visible even in the dim light.

"Steve says I have to tell Endora the truth," he said. "He says if I don't, he will."

"It's because of Kaye," Lila told him. "Your grandmother fired her today."

"I know. But you'd think I would take precedent over some maid, wouldn't you?"

Lila laughed softly. The perfume from the wisteria drifted by her nose in the slight breeze, and all around was the rustle of the eucalyptus leaves. She withdrew her hand from Jay's grasp.

"What are you laughing at?" he asked sullenly.

"I'm laughing at you."

"Thanks a lot. Talk about kicking a man when he's down—"

Lila laughed again. "Honestly, Jay, you're a panic, you really are."

"What do you mean?"

"Well, here you are, a grown man. You have good looks and a quick mind on your side, but do you use them for anything more than taking advantage of people? No, you do not. And then when you get caught at your nasty little games, you act like a wounded puppy and expect everyone to cover for you as though you were a small child."

"I know I have to accept my punishment," he said. "I'm willing to leave for a while."

"See? You expect to be slapped on the wrist when the truth of the matter is that you caused an honest woman to lose not only her job, but her dignity and her employer's trust as well. Those are intangible things impossible to put a price on, and you took them from Kaye without even batting one of your attractive eyelashes. For stealing and forging your grandmother's name, you could end up in prison. She would never press those kinds of charges, and you know it, so you took advantage of her love for you to steal from her. It doesn't matter if she can afford it or not—that's not the issue. Steven's right—when are you going to grow up?''

Jay shrugged. ''I guess I'm going to grow up tonight, because that's the deadline Steven has imposed for confessing all my sins to Grandmother.''

''It takes more than one confession,'' Lila said softly. She touched his chest over his heart and said, ''Try using this once in a while too.''

''I tried using my heart with you, Lila,'' Jay said, ''and look where it got me.''

Lila smiled indulgently. *More games,* she thought, but she didn't say it. Changes don't come overnight, and she had a feeling Jay had yet to grasp the reality of his situation. He would, she thought, and for a second wished she could be a fly on the wall when he told Endora the truth. The moment passed, and she changed her mind. Better to scurry upstairs, putting as much distance as possible between her and the scene that would unfold over the rest of the evening.

The coatdress was straight and daffodil yellow. It had a scooped neck and self-covered buttons that ran from the neckline to six inches above the hem. Lila thought it brought out the brown of her eyes and the shining cap of dark hair she thought were her best features. As she studied her reflection, she saw that she did rather look like Aunt Connie, a resemblance that pleased her.

She'd spent the night painting with the quick-drying water-based acrylics she'd taken from her trunk before retreating upstairs the night before. She'd spent the morning sitting by her window, waiting to catch a glimpse of Steven crossing from the guest house to the main house. In fact, she'd almost fallen asleep waiting for him to appear from the trees, and when he finally did, her gaze stayed on him. So intense was her staring that she fully expected him to "feel" her looking, and when he didn't glance up toward her window, she felt disappointed. Maybe he really didn't love her.

Meanwhile the house was alive with sounds. She could hear Endora's booming voice as well as a few unfamiliar voices, which suggested guests were beginning to arrive. Lila felt displaced, a stranger among friends. She wondered if she should have stayed this long. She wondered where she was going to go tomorrow. While it was true she had a little money, she didn't have a job, nor did she have the experience to secure one easily. Well, life was a struggle, and tomorrow morning her struggle began. She just hoped she didn't have a broken heart to cope with as well, because if there was one thing she'd discovered during the night, it was this—it was too late. She was already in love.

She was tired of questions and uncertainty but too chicken to go downstairs and see what had transpired during the night, so she hid in her room, away from the hustle and bustle of party preparations. All week long, cases of champagne, crates of fresh food, and vases of flowers had been arriving, and Lila assumed Rose and Endora were directing Steven and Jay in the proper dispersal of everything. Or was Jay already gone?

She tiptoed across the hall and from the open door peeked into his room. It was as neat as a pin, impossible to tell if he was still living in it without actually opening drawers and closets, which she most certainly wasn't about to do. At last, her stomach protesting the missed breakfast, she walked back into her own room, collected Endora's present, and went down the stairs.

"Is that for me?" Endora cried.

"Yes."

"Oh, you shouldn't have. Here, I'll take it and put it with my other presents. Isn't this fun? Now, Lila, tell me the truth. I just couldn't face that gown again. What do you think of this?" She turned around slowly, showing off yet another purple dress, this one more blue than red and with a high neckline, multiple floating ruffles, and a huge corsage of lilacs pinned to the bosom.

"You look spectacular," Lila told her, taking Endora's free hand. She kissed the wrinkled cheek, which reeked of lilac scent, and added, "Happy birthday!"

"Thank you," Endora said. She lowered her eyes and added, "Jay told me about Kaye, about how he took the money, not her. I called her and groveled all over the place. She said she might come back, that she's thinking about it."

"She'll come back," Lila said. "She likes you very much."

"If she comes back, it will be because of the raise I bribed her with! Well, I refuse to think about this matter right now, that's all. I have guests coming!"

As if to punctuate this remark, the doorbell rang. Lila turned to face the door and saw Jay answering it. She looked back at Endora, who said simply, "He's my grandson. Someday, when you have children of your own, you'll understand."

Lila nodded. When Jay looked her way, she smiled at him and wasn't too surprised when he winked at her. Jay bounced back, all right, but Lila felt herself wondering just how honest he'd been with Endora. She craned her neck to peer into the study and drawing room, but though there were a few strangers milling around, she caught no sight of Steven.

By the time one o'clock rolled around, the house was bustling with people. Endora introduced her agent, a tall woman with a firm handshake and strong facial features. She had a tight coil of impossibly red hair, vivid green eyes, and a gaze that looked as though it could see through lead. Lila wondered how the woman hadn't seen through *Murder in Neon*.

The main table was spread with cold sliced meats, masses of fresh fruit and vegetables, cheeses, hot dishes, breads, lilac-colored gladiolus, mums, stock, and—of course—lilacs. The centerpiece was an ice sculpture, which Lila stared at for quite a while until she finally figured out that it was supposed to resemble Endora. The warm day was accelerating the melting process, and Lila wondered how long it would be before the centerpiece would be reduced to a bowl of ice water.

As Lila filled a plate and tried not to look for Steven, she saw Edward Booker approaching. ''Quite a party,'' he said. He said it loud because the dining-room windows opened directly onto the back patio, where a small band had just begun to play. Waiters, who had come with the caterer—even Endora didn't expect Cook and Rose to handle all this food and service by themselves—scurried inside and out with trays full of hors d'oeuvres and champagne.

''Endora is having a ball,'' Lila said.

Edward snatched a stuffed mushroom cap from the table and popped it into his mouth. After he swallowed, he said, ''I've been thinking about things since last night, and I've decided to do a retrospective of Constance's work. Would you be willing to help me put it together?''

For one brief second Lila wanted to pour champagne on his foot, but she swallowed the last remnants of bitterness and said, ''Sure, why not?''

''And I'd like to include you in the piece as well. Kind of the carry-on-the-torch angle—you know what I mean?''

''I think so, but I don't know if I want to do that.''

''Listen, young lady. I know what you think of my magazine, and I don't blame you, but print is print, and publicity is publicity. I happen to know Endora gave a sneak preview of your painting to an art critic here in town who was absolutely enchanted with your work and wants to help you mount a show. We could use that—"

Lila had just seen Steven enter the back door. "Later, okay?" she told Edward and, putting her untouched plate aside, made her way through the crowd to intercept Steven's path.

His smile upon seeing her spoke volumes and set Lila's heart on fire. He took her hand and raised it to his lips, kissing her fingers as though they were alone and not in the crush of a merrymaking crowd. "I've been thinking about you all morning," he said as he guided her toward a relatively quiet corner of the dining room.

"Me too."

"We have to talk."

"I know."

"Because for better or worse, I love you, Lila Greene. What do I need a leaky tub for when I have you? Do I have you, Lila?"

"You certainly do, but, Steven—"

"I don't know what the future holds—"

"Who does?"

"One thing I do know. I will never stand in the way of your career."

"Steven, there will be a way to work this out, I just know it."

"There's nothing to work out," he insisted. "I've made my decision."

"But, Steven—"

"I do love you," he said. "Very much."

Lila stood on the tips of her toes and kissed him

quickly on the lips. "I love you too," she said. She felt his arms go around her waist, lifting her from the floor—

A loud bell rang through the house, and Rose appeared at Lila's elbow. "She wants you two," Rose said. "In the drawing room, now."

"The big unveiling?" Steven asked as he lowered Lila to the floor.

"Yep. I'd hurry if I were you."

Lila reached for Steven's hand, but they became separated in the crowd, so she made her way to the front of the house until Endora saw her and called out, "Make room for my artist, everyone. Make room."

She felt like Moses parting the Red Sea as the crowd stepped aside and she joined Endora. She took her first deep breath and was assailed by the smell of lilacs; Endora had wielded a heavy hand when she sprayed the room earlier, and now with the body heat of the crowd, even the open windows couldn't help.

The easel was behind Endora, cleverly covered so that no material touched the still-wet paint. A table stacked with birthday gifts was off to Endora's left. One exquisitely wrapped present towered above the rest. The paper was lilac, of course, and the bow was actually a cluster of silk lilacs with bright-green leaves.

"Where's Steven?" Endora asked.

Lila pointed to the back of the room. "Right there, see?" He waved and Endora waved back.

"I wanted him to be closer, but I suppose that will have to do. Jay is over there with my agent. Probably flirting with her."

"She's old enough to be his mother—"

"She's old enough to enjoy the attentions of a younger man," Endora said, chuckling. "Let her have her fun for a while. I just hope she watches her purse."

Lila covered her mouth with her hand and decided she didn't have to worry about Endora.

"Everyone?" Endora cried, and after repeating it three times, the crowd quieted down. Endora said, "First off, thank you all for coming. Most of you are dear friends, and as some of you older ones know, when you get to be my age, you begin counting friends on one hand. I'm blessed."

A healthy round of applause. Lila clapped politely as her gaze stayed glued to Steven's. She hoped Endora got this thing over with quickly so she and Steven could get back to what they'd been doing! There was so much they had to talk about—

"Before I unveil my portrait, I'm going to open my presents." A chair was produced, and Lila found herself in the position of helping Endora unwrap all her gifts. Endora loved the amethyst pendant Steven had given her and insisted on wearing it. It immediately got lost in the ruffles, but the polite gathering oohed appreciatively, anyway.

She opened Lila's gift next and, for once, was speechless. She turned it to show her guests, and a round of applause broke the silence. Lila had painted it in acrylics the night before on a small canvas. It was a picture of Jay and Steven standing on the bluff, Steven gazing out toward the sea, Jay smiling straight ahead.

She finally came to the last present, which was the beautifully wrapped lilac box. She set it on her lap and said, "This is my present to myself and to my boys."

This statement got the people buzzing, but the noise died down as she opened the lid and took out a narrow folder of papers.

"Two tickets on the Queen Elizabeth, departing from New York in June and not returning until six months later!" She waved them. People laughed, but Lila's and Steven's eyes met, confused. Did Endora believe she could send Steven and Jay away together?

"Grandmother," Jay said during a lull. "I can't go to England—"

"They're not for you," Endora interrupted, her eyes sparkling. "They're for me and Rose. Rose, where are you, dear?"

Rose, as always, was close at hand. "Me, really?" she asked, tears glistening in her eyes.

"Of course," Endora said, putting her arm around her servant's—and friend's—shoulder. "We're going to go on an adventure, just like one of my heroines. Who knows, Rose? We may fall in love with a couple of dashing octogenarians!"

Laughter filled the room. Lila grinned at Steven, who looked baffled.

"Wait a minute," Endora's agent said.

"What is it, Fran?"

"What about your books? I was here to offer you a contract on your next three—"

"Talk to Steven," Endora said with an imperious wave of her hand.

"Steven? Endora, you can't just run away—"

"I'm doing exactly that," Endora said firmly. "I've decided to retire. I've decided to let Steven take over the writing for the Yolette family. No doubt he'll do it from aboard that boat of his, but what with fax machines and computers and things . . . and as for contracts, I'd like you to know, Fran, that Steven wrote *Murder in Neon*, or at least most of it; the germ of the idea was mine, of course. What's more, I believe he has just completed another book, or at least I hope he has. He's certainly been busy on something." She winked at Steven, who looked as though he could be knocked over with a feather. Then she looked at Jay.

"As for you, my handsome one, I've decided to leave you some of your inheritance early. You can go to school, travel, gamble it away, I don't care. But until I die of old age—which I don't expect to do for quite a while yet—it's all you'll get. Now, what have I forgotten?"

When Endora's gaze landed on Lila, Lila shook her head. She had no idea what else the woman had planned. She wasn't sure her grandsons, or the rest of the crowd, were ready for any more.

"How about the portrait?" Steven called out.

"I did that already, didn't I?" She turned around, saw the still-veiled canvas, and laughed at herself. "Do you see, Fran? That's why it's time to retire. I forget things all the time. Luckily Rose has the mind of a twenty-year-old, so she ought to be able to keep track of me. . . . Where was I?"

"The portrait," Rose said, and everyone laughed.

"Oh, of course, my portrait! I was going to do that first, but I seemed to have gotten distracted. You all have these little cards with Lila's name that Rose passed out at the door? Good, let me explain." As everyone waited, Endora related the story of how she had hired Constance Greene to paint her portrait—not really true, Lila thought—but that since she was dead (ever tactful), Lila had taken the job and that she, Endora Yolette, couldn't be more thrilled with the results. Lila helped her lift the veil, and there was the portrait.

Lila would long remember the reaction of the crowd—hushed silence, murmurs, a shout of "Bravo!" from an opera buff in the back, then thunderous applause.

Endora quieted everyone. "I am sensible enough to know you're not carrying on because I'm such a tantalizing old dish, though, believe me, I was a few years ago. You're all excited because you're witnessing the birth of a great new artist, Lila Greene!"

More applause. Lila, not given to blushing, blushed. She bet her face looked like a strawberry or a tomato or, better yet, as though it had been dipped in a tub of crimson paint.

A stranger appeared before her. He was a small, round man with a preposterous mustache that, save for a pair of faint eyebrows and a couple of stubby eyelashes, constituted the only hair on his head.

Endora quieted everyone down again. "This is Calvin Cluster, Lila," she said in her best stage voice. "He wants to help you." Lila's jaw dropped. She'd heard of Calvin Cluster—who in the art world hadn't? He was the maker of young artists' dreams and careers.

"I have great hope for your future, young lady," he said. "I have a small studio where I am prepared to offer you employment. Working together, we will make the name Lila Greene equally as respected as that of Constance Greene. I will help shape your destiny!" he finished with a dramatic flourish.

Still more applause.

"Now, don't be angry," Endora confided to Lila, "but I did it again."

"Did what?"

"I showed Calvin your drawings. Oh, don't look at me like that, Lila, I only did it to help. You're too modest. If there's anything I abhor, it's false modesty."

"But, Endora—"

"You drew a lot of pictures of Steven," she said.

"Well—"

"Lovely pictures, tender pictures. In fact, I don't believe I ever realized how handsome he is until I saw him through your eyes, Lila. They truly comprise a portrait of love."

Lila nodded, completely overwhelmed.

"Oh, and while I searched for your drawings, I found my book *Call of the Wind*. It was there on the desk in your room. Did you like it?"

Lila swallowed. "Yes," she said.

"Good. I reread parts of it. Incredible how well I remembered it, isn't it? You would have thought I wrote it yesterday and not thirty years ago. Of course, Steven helped me along by jogging my memory.''

"I'm sorry," Lila said. "He didn't know what to do—"

"I know that, dear. I'm not even going to waste time being embarrassed. Not that I exactly want the story spread hither and yon, but an old woman has a right to a few eccentricities, doesn't she?''

Lila laughed. She searched the crowd of faces for Steven and felt the first alarming tingle of fear when she couldn't find him. Then she was swamped with people congratulating her and, with Endora's arm looped possessively through hers, was unable to investigate. In fact, by the time she was able to break free, almost an hour had passed. She made her way through the house without finding him anywhere.

He wasn't at the guest house, either, but as she walked back to the main house, her heart soared. He was standing by the bluff.

The illusion lasted only a fraction of a second. It wasn't Steven standing there; it was Jay. He looked over his shoulder and waved her over. Lila would have loved to duck out of seeing him right then, but there was no polite way to do it, so she joined him.

"Quite a day for you and Steve," he said.

Lila smiled. "Have you seen him?"

"He took off a while ago. Did you know he was writing Grandmother's books?"

"Yes, I knew, but he only wrote her last one, *Murder in Neon*."

"I had no idea."

This disclosure didn't surprise Lila. If a matter didn't directly concern Jay, it didn't matter to him. She took a step toward the house, anxious to find Steven.

''She publicly humiliated me,'' he said. ''She as much as told people I'd been mooching off her.''

''She cut the lines and pushed you out to sea,'' Lila said. ''She was much kinder to you than you had a right to expect. I think it'll be good for you.''

''At least I'll be rich for a while,'' he mumbled, and Lila, tired of his company, walked away.

The next person to catch her attention was Fran. ''Where's Endora's grandson? Not him,'' she said as Lila unconsciously looked toward Jay. ''The talented one. My next big writer!''

''I'm not sure,'' Lila told her.

''If you see him, tell him I need to talk to him tonight or tomorrow morning before ten. My plane leaves at noon,'' she explained.

''I'll tell him,'' Lila promised. She made her way in the door, ran upstairs for her purse, then lost time dodging Calvin Cluster as she tried to get out the front door. It took a deep breath before she was ready to tackle the arduous chore of freeing her little red car, but finally she was on the road heading to the Shelter Island Yacht Club.

She'd never been there without a member before, so it took some quick talking to get the guard to let her through the gate. She drove around to the marina, parked, and fairly flew down the dock toward *Ariel*.

''I knew you'd be here,'' she said from the dock.

Steven was stretched out in the cockpit. He looked at Lila and said, "Come aboard."

She had to unbutton the last three buttons of her dress before she could make the wide step from the dock to *Ariel*'s deck. She sat down opposite Steven and said, "You look like a man who is saying good-bye to something he loves."

He sat up. "I'm not quite that melodramatic. I just wanted to think, that's all. A boat is a great place to think." He took her hands in his and added, "I'm sorry I left without telling you."

"Honestly, Steven. You've been acting like an advertisement for reliability for over a year now, and just when I need you to remain reasonable, you turn all emotional on me."

"What?"

"Why did you run away? Was it because of Endora? Fran wants to see you, and I talked with your grand-mother. She knows about *Call of the Wind*, and though she's a little embarrassed at her own lapse, she's genuinely touched that you tried to shield her from it. She found out because I left the book on my desk, and while she was snooping around looking for draw-ings—"

"It's not the writing," he interrupted. "In fact, I can't tell you what a relief it is to have that over with."

"Then what?"

"You know I love you; that's no secret. And today you were handed the opportunity of a lifetime."

"And you were given your freedom," Lila said.

"That doesn't matter. Lila, I'll be honest with you.

I've been fighting falling in love with you since the first time I laid eyes on your beautiful face. A few nights ago I spent hours brooding on the back patio, telling myself I didn't need you, that when I got free of my responsibilities with Endora—

"Well, it doesn't matter. I almost convinced myself, but then I chanced to look up toward your window, and I thought I saw your face. It took my breath away. Well, love is fickle, and when it strikes, it strikes. I'm not going to run anymore. Like I said earlier, I love you, and that's that. What matters now is your art. I've said that all along."

"And what about yours?"

"You mean writing? I can do that anywhere."

"Could you do it aboard *Ariel*?"

"Yes, of course—"

"Because that's what I was trying to tell you earlier at the party when you kept interrupting me. I adore this boat. I think sailing her around the world sounds like heaven, and furthermore, I think I could paint aboard her. I'd use smaller canvases, of course. I already tried switching to acrylics, and it worked fine. Would you be able to make a place for me to work in? It might take some refinement, say, of the forepeak. Is that what you call that first cabin up there?"

"Yes, but, honey, you're not thinking."

"It seems to me as though I am."

"But Calvin Cluster—"

"Is offering me a jail term. He's offering me years of hard work under his wise tutelage. Well, I've already had that with Aunt Connie, and with all due respect to

Calvin, I'm not anxious to do it again. I loved my aunt, Steven, and caring for her was a labor of love. But now it's over, and all I want is to be free to paint on my own terms.''

''Is that all you want?'' he asked softly.

Lila smiled. ''No. I want you. I want to sail around the world on *Ariel*. I want you. Did I already mention that?''

''I believe so,'' he whispered as his lips touched hers.

Chapter Eleven

Lila held her left hand out in front of her. The wide
gold band pleased her. She'd been wearing it only six
hours, but it already felt familiar, like a part of her.

"Mrs. Yolette? Will you please get your pretty self
up here and lend me a hand?"

Lila darted up the companionway ladder. *Ariel* was
ready to go, and she knew Steven was anxious because
Endora hadn't shown up yet and she'd promised to
come see them off.

She found him straddling the main boom, sitting atop
the mainsail, which was all folded down, his bare feet
hanging in midair above the cabin top. He was working
on a piece of sail track, replacing a stainless screw.
He was always finding something to tinker with or
replace or repair. She wondered if he was ever going

to get his book written, what with all the distractions *Ariel* provided.

"Hand me that fat screwdriver, will you?" he asked. He'd taken off his shirt, and his brown skin glistened. She searched his toolbox, found the right screwdriver, and handed it to him. "A kiss?" he asked.

She kissed his knee.

"That's not what I meant."

"You just get this tub ready to go. Where's your grandmother?"

Steven looked down the dock, and Lila saw his handsome face break into a grin. "Look," he said.

There she was, coming down the dock, decked out in purple from her head to her toes. The wind fluttered her dress and hat, while the act of walking jangled her bracelets; the scent of lilacs seemed to waft down the dock ahead of her.

"Darling children," she called. Lila saw Rose had come too, and so had Mr. Cook. They were both bearing boxes, and Lila sighed as she wondered where she was going to stow anything else. The forepeak was crammed with her painting supplies; the aft cabin was cluttered with writing things.

It took some doing, but eventually they got Endora aboard. She sat in the cockpit, one eye hidden by the dashing tilt of the brim of her floppy hat. Rose handed Lila the boxes, and as Lila unpacked them, she found all sorts of treasures, from flowers—not lilacs, but lilac-colored roses—to chilled champagne and cooked lobster. On the bottom of one of the boxes was a new can of lilac-scented air freshener.

"That's for ambience," Endora called, her face framed in the companionway hatch. "The rest is your honeymoon feast."

Lila went back into the cockpit and hugged Endora. "Almost everything is edible," she said.

"Steven told me if I gave either one of you anything else you had to find a place for, he'd throttle me."

"In the nicest possible way," Steven said, pulling on his shirt. "When are you ladies off for New York?"

"The day after tomorrow," Rose said, her face reflecting the excitement she kept in tight control. She looked at Cook and added, "Guess who's coming with us?"

"You, Mr. Cook?"

"Mrs. Yolette asked me," he said, grinning.

"Think how excited all the old ladies on that boat are going to be when Cook shows up!" Endora said. She smiled at the sight of Steven perched on the coaming next to Lila, his hand resting casually on her shoulder. "Haven't I always said you two looked adorable together?" she cooed. "Okay, now for business. Steven, Fran called me after the wedding this morning and said the second printing of *Murder in Neon* will feature both our names. She also said that she loves your new book and already has a couple of publishers interested and that she's thinking of trying to convince someone to reprint *Call of the Wind* with the few modest changes I made this time around. And, Lila, Calvin called again. This time I'm to tell you that you are to send him your paintings as you flit about the world and that you are to call him the minute your marriage breaks up or you get back here.''

"This marriage is not going to break up," Steven said.

"I know, dear, but I didn't have the heart to tell him. Well, now, my darlings, I have to go. The real-estate people are bringing by the couple who are going to rent the house while we're away. I must make sure they know how to take care of the lilacs. Of course, Kaye will be there to help, and the gardener, but still, one likes to be prepared. Rose? Cook?''

"I'm going to miss you," Steven said as he kissed his grandmother good-bye. They were standing on the dock.

"I know, dear, but I have faith Lila will keep you diverted. Besides, when you come back, perhaps you'll stay with me. Think of the house as a great, big mooring buoy, will you, and come back someday?''

Lila smiled, suddenly choked with tears. She hated saying good-bye. She hugged Endora, whispered her thanks, then asked, "What about Jay? Have you heard from him lately?''

"Last word was a postcard from Rio. Don't you worry about that charming grandson of mine. He's a survivor. Bon voyage, darlings.''

Arm in arm, Steven and Lila stood on the foredeck and watched Endora walk up the dock. When she disappeared from view, Steven kissed the top of Lila's head. "Well, Mrs. Yolette, shall we sail off toward the sunset or find a private anchorage for our wedding night?''

Lila voted for the anchorage. As Steven started the engine to get the boat away from the dock, she placed the roses in a coffeepot full of water. She glanced at the bulkhead, at Aunt Connie's small painting of Lila done a lifetime before, then down at the gold ring on her finger. Steven would need help with the dock lines, she realized, and, propping the flowers in the sink, she went back on deck.